LETHAL LEFTOVERS

Jane inched her way carefully, making small sweeps of the ground with her flashlight in search of her lost watch. "Here it is!" she called. "Thank goodness! I wonder if it still— Oh, my God!"

She'd held the watch up to her ear with her left hand while ignoring where the beam from the flashlight was pointing.

"What's wrong?" Shelley asked.

Jane stood frozen and speechless for a moment, then whispered, "Shelley, there's a body here!"

Jane Jeffry Mysteries by
Jill Churchill
from Avon Books

JILL CHURCHILL

Fear of Frying

A JANE JEFFRY MYSTERY

AVON BOOKS
An Imprint of HarperCollinsPublishers

You can email Jill Churchill at Cozybooks@aol.com

AVON BOOKS
An Imprint of HarperCollins*Publishers*
10 East 53rd Street
New York, New York 10022-5299

Copyright © 1997 by The Janice Young Brooks Trust
Excerpts from *Grime and Punishment* copyright © 1989 by Janice Young Brooks; *A Farewell to Yarns* copyright © 1991 by Janice Young Brooks; *A Quiche Before Dying* copyright © 1993 by The Janice Young Brooks Trust; *The Class Menagerie* copyright © 1994 by the Janice Young Brooks Trust; *A Knife to Remember* copyright © 1994 by The Janice Young Brooks Trust; *From Here to Paternity* copyright © 1995 by The Janice Young Brooks Trust; *Silence of the Hams* copyright © 1996 by The Janice Young Brooks Trust
Inside cover author photo by Stephen Locke Portraits
www.avonbooks.com
Library of Congress Catalog Card Number: 97-3188
ISBN: 0-380-78707-5

First Avon Twilight printing: November 1998
First Avon Books hardcover printing: November 1997

Avon Trademark Reg. U.S. Pat. Off. and in Other Countries, Marca Registrada, Hecho en U.S.A.
HarperCollins® is a trademark of HarperCollins Publishers Inc.

Printed in the U.S.A.

10 9 8 7 6 5

For Faith
with many thanks

One

❖❖ "Horse blinders," Jane Jeffry said. "That's what
❖ I need when you're driving. Horse blinders. With
a flap that comes down in front, too. So all I can see
is my lap."

Jane's best friend, Shelley Nowack, eased her foot
off the gas pedal. The van slowed slightly. "I've
never had an accident," Shelley said. "Not even one
that wasn't my fault."

"I don't find that encouraging. It only means all
your bad luck is being saved for a really big one.
And as dear as you are to me, I don't want to be
with you when you have it."

"Just play with your computer and don't look outside," Shelley said, swinging out around an eighteen-
wheeler as if it were no more of an obstacle than
a Honda.

Jane patted the top of the screen of her laptop. It
was a recent gift from her parents. Her father was
with the State Department, and they moved from
country to country as frequently and easily as Jane
went to the grocery store—and a lot more cheerfully.

Her father had called from Finland to tell her it was coming. "E-mail, Jane," he'd said. "I figure I'll save the cost of the computers in long-distance bills in a year."

"Computers, plural?" Jane had asked.

"Mike's getting one, too," he'd said.

Mike was Jane's son, in his freshman year at college. Since Jane was widowed several years earlier, Mike—who was one of the rarest elements in the universe, a relatively sensible teenager—had been a great support to her. Now that he was away, she was missing him like mad. But Mike didn't want to have his dorm-mates overhear him talking to his mother on the phone, and except for the obligatory thank-you notes and college applications she'd forced him to produce, he'd never spontaneously written a letter in his life. But E-mail, in the two weeks they'd had their laptops, had provided the solution. And Jane had also enjoyed more correspondence with her parents in that time than they'd had for years.

Just now, however, she and the laptop were engaged in a hot game of gin rummy. And even though she was losing badly, it was better than watching the scenery flash by at a terrifying rate.

"You brought your new boots, didn't you?" Shelley said, almost accusingly.

"The ones you called 'shit-kickers'? Of course. They're actually pretty comfortable, but if you think I'm going to kick shit or anything else with them, you're mistaken. You promised me this trip wasn't anything like . . . camping." She pronounced the last word with a shudder. "I went camping once. I was fourteen and I got ticks in my hair. I'm still trying to get over it. Humankind has spent hundreds of generations developing indoor plumbing. I think it's flying in the face of progress to pee in the woods.''

"Jane, I've told you this isn't a 'pee in the woods' kind of camp. We'll have our own little cabin with a bathroom. There's even a fireplace. It's more like a somewhat rustic resort.''

"But no kitchen, right? You promised me there wouldn't be a kitchen.''

"No kitchen. This is a camp for kids, and nobody wants them to do any cooking.''

"There aren't going to be kids there with us, are there?'' Jane asked, turning off the laptop and wondering if the computer cheated or whether she just stunk at card games.

"No kids. I don't think you've paid attention to anything I've told you.''

"Shelley, I was just glad to get a little vacation. And I didn't know there was going to be a test. So tell me again.''

Shelley sighed. "The town council and the school district got together to sponsor a summer-school camp for kids and have researched a ton of them. This one in Wisconsin looks like the best bet, was easy to get to from Chicago, and the best deal for the town financially. Plus, this resort is the one that put the idea in their heads by proposing the plan in the first place. But the council and school board wanted some parents to come check it out firsthand and make a report. I managed to get us in as one of the 'couples.' ''

"So what are we supposed to do?''

"Whatever we want,'' Shelley said. "Or as little

as we want. The camp has all sorts of activities—craft stuff, hiking trails, even one of those tough 'boot camp' type programs where you crawl through swamps and climb cliffs."

"There are swamps in Wisconsin?"

"I don't know. Maybe they built one. I think there are bogs, whatever they are. But we don't have to do that."

"You bet we don't!" Jane said. "You'd have to hold a gun to my head to get me to crawl through a swamp—or a bog—for fun!"

"I think they've adapted it a bit for adults. Just as a demonstration, we're all going to a campfire cooking class tomorrow night, I'm told."

"Oh, no! Shelley, cooking was one of the things I thought I was getting a vacation *from*."

"We don't have to cook. At least I don't think so. Just listen to someone telling us about cooking. And then we get to taste the samples when it's over. You like tasting stuff, Jane. It'll be fun."

They were approaching an interchange. Shelley glanced up at the directions she'd stuck on her sun visor and zipped into the right lane, nearly running a tour bus off the road. "It's not far now. We can stop here, get some coffee, go to the bathroom—"

"Why do we need to go to the bathroom here?" Jane asked suspiciously. "Can't we go when we get to the camp? Shelley, are you hiding something from me? We *are* going to have to pee in the woods, aren't we!"

They left the interstate, took a nice four-lane highway for thirty miles, then turned off on a two-lane for another twenty. They missed the turnoff for the county road and had to backtrack a mile or two. This led them into a lushly wooded area. The road curved, dipped, and occasionally crested a rise, revealing tantalizing views of hills brilliant with autumn coloring and the fleeting impression of sun on sparkling little lakes. Out of deference to both Jane's nerves and the beauty of the landscape, Shelley actually slowed down to a normal driving speed.

"About another mile," Shelley finally said. "Watch for a sign on the right."

Jane was encouraged by the sign. It said CAMP SUNSHINE and was large and freshly painted. She'd imagined it would be an old wooden plank with the words scribbled in charcoal and leading to something that looked like the Bates Motel.

They crossed over a picturesque wood-slatted bridge and onto a road, freshly graveled and recently traveled, judging by the haze of white dust drifting above the surface. "Who else is coming?" she asked.

"I'm not sure," Shelley said. "There were a couple of last-minute changes. The Wilsons, who run the bakery, were signed up, but she had to have emergency gall bladder surgery last week, so somebody will have replaced them. And the Youngbloods had to cancel because he's changing jobs and they had to go look at houses in Buffalo. The Claypool brothers and their wives are coming, I think."

"Who are they?"

"Oh, Jane. You know them. They have that huge car dealership."

"I recognize the name, but I don't think I've ever

met them. They're not going to try to sell us cars, are they?''

"It wouldn't be a bad thing if somebody sold you a car," Shelley said. "That station wagon of yours is starting to sound like a blender with a walnut inside when you start it."

"True, but it still starts. Most of the time."

Shelley just shook her head. "You should know Marge Claypool. She does a lot of volunteer work. She was on the committee for the Well Baby clinic."

"I wasn't involved in that as much as you were. I don't remember her."

"Well, you wouldn't, I guess. She's a worker bee. Never speaks up, never has any fresh ideas, but will do anything she's assigned and do it well and without seeming to want any recognition."

"What a paragon!"

"Yes, but she's very nice. I ran into her last week in the grocery store and she was all bubbly about this vacation. Apparently neither family has had any sort of vacation for years. The brothers have very difficult, demanding, elderly parents who should be in a retirement home, but refuse to go. The parents have an old house, both need constant medical care and a housekeeper and cook. According to Marge, they treat everybody she and Sam hire for them like medieval serfs and can't keep anyone more than a month or two. She didn't put it in those words, but it was easy to read between the lines. So her husband and his brother—and of course, their wives—are constantly on duty, having to replace people. I guess one of them finally put his foot down and decided they'd take some time off—no matter what."

"So who are the brothers?"

"Marge's husband is Sam. I think he's the older one. He seems more like a college professor than a car dealer. Kind of prissy. The other is John, who's a glad-hander. I've only met him once and wasn't crazy about him. Cheerful, but real brash and loud."

"Who else?" Jane asked.

"I'm not sure. Somebody from the school board and somebody from the city council. Ah, here we are."

They turned at another freshly painted sign. The drive was narrow and wound through a thick stand of pines. Autumn wildflowers bloomed at the side of the road. As they rounded the last curve, they saw a large building that resembled an overgrown log cabin. It was two stories high and had a porch across the front with some ancient rocking chairs set about in companionable groupings. The building looked old—as if it had been part of the landscape for decades. The logs from which it was constructed were covered with bark. Lichen and moss grew on the logs, and tender-looking ferns clustered close to the building.

"Golly!" Jane said as Shelley pulled the van up in front of the entrance. "What a neat place." As they stepped out of the car, Jane breathed deeply. "Real pine scent! And there's a campfire somewhere. Can you smell it?"

"Take a look around," Shelley said, rummaging in her purse for her paperwork. "I'll get us checked in."

Jane strolled along the porch, testing a couple of the rocking chairs. "I could sit here for hours just drinking this air," she said out loud, startling a woodpecker who'd been tapping furiously on the building. This struck her as appropriately rustic, even though a woodpecker at her own house had once driven her nearly to frenzy.

Shelley was back in a minute. "Nobody at the desk," she said, "but I found this on the bulletin board." She'd removed two keys and a map from an envelope. "Hop in the van."

"We're not staying here?"

"No, there are cabins down the road. We're looking for Happy Memories."

"Sure we are. Isn't everybody?"

"Jane, don't be a smart aleck. That's the name of the cabin."

"The name of the cabin? Happy Memories? That's so horribly *cute* I don't think I can stand it!"

"It's on the right, but not for a bit," Shelley said, putting the van in gear and heading down a narrow, pine-shaded drive that ran at right angles to the road they'd come in on. Little rustic signposts identified the driveways to cabins, some of which weren't even visible from the road. SUMMER'S END, HOME AGAIN, DEER RUN VIEW, and finally HAPPY MEMORIES.

"Oh, Shelley!" Jane sighed at the sight of the cabin. It was a tiny version of the main lodge building—neatly fitted logs with rough bark, a beautifully mossy wood-shake roof hugged by overhanging branches, spots of bright fall wildflowers in the surrounding woods.

They pulled in and hopped out of the van. The surprisingly modern lock on the door worked easily. The interior was extremely "cabinish" with knotty pine walls and a wood floor scattered with braided rugs in soothing, muted colors. The furniture—two single beds, a couple of tables, and a pair of deeply cushioned chairs with afghans tossed over the backs—was primitive. So was the stone hearth around the fireplace. But to Jane's surprise, the entire far wall was all glass, floor-to-ceiling windows, with French doors leading to a back porch the width of the cabin. Three more rocking chairs like the one at the main building sat glowing in the late afternoon sun. There was fireplace wood stacked at the end of the porch, just waiting to become a cozy fire.

Jane went out on the porch, which hung out over a steep incline. Below, a small creek burbled past, and above her, birds warbled. A squirrel leaped from one tree to another, swinging wildly on the branch. "Shelley, this is really heaven— Shelley?"

Jane went inside, just as Shelley came in the other door laden with her belongings. "Which bed do you want?" she asked.

"The one nearest the porch, if that's okay. What is all that stuff?"

"The necessities of life," Shelley said, unloading a hair dryer, lighted makeup mirror, hot rollers, and coffeemaker.

"Uh-huh," Jane said. "There might be a small problem, Shelley." She pointed at the small kerosene lamp sitting on the table between the beds, and the other one on the table on the far wall. "There don't seem to be any electrical outlets."

Shelley stared at Jane blankly, then stared at the kerosene lamps, looked at the ceiling, hoping in vain to see an overhead light. Then she sat down on the bed, among her appliances. "Oh, Jane. I'll *die* without electricity! What have I done to us?"

Two

❖❖ Shelley ran outside, looked around, and came
 ❖ back in, saying accusingly, "There are wires
coming into the cabin, so there must be electricity."

"Probably just phone lines," Jane said, pointing
to a telephone sitting on a tiny table. Shelley was so
seldom rattled about anything that it was a pleasure
to see her scrambling around looking for electricity.
But Jane was a little concerned, too. She'd planned
on using her laptop to keep in touch with the kids
and with her "significant other" (a phrase she hated,
but her teenage daughter was mortified by the con-
cept of her mother having a "boyfriend," and Jane
had reluctantly adopted Katie's preferred modern ter-
minology), Mel VanDyne, via modem. But while the
laptop had a battery, it probably didn't have enough
juice to last for several days. Still, there would certainly be power in the main lodge where she could
recharge it, while Shelley would look pretty silly
using the lodge to dry and curl her hair and put on
her makeup.

While Shelley got progressively more frantic in

her search, Jane explored the rest of the cabin. It was
rectangular with a large section taken out on the
north wall. The first door into this section revealed
a tiny storage room with extra blankets and pillows
and a lot of fishing gear. Minnow buckets, life preservers, a selection of elderly fishing poles, and a
tackle box. She closed that door and tried the other,
which was the bathroom.

And what a bathroom! "Shelley!" Jane exclaimed.
"Get a look at this!"

There was a large, deep tub with water-jet hard-
ware, a double sink, and a separate area that had a
very modern toilet and glass-enclosed shower. Jane
stared for a moment before realizing she had reflex-
ively flipped on the light switch when she entered
the room.

"Lights! Electricity!" Shelley exclaimed. Then
she started laughing. "Talk about selective renovations! What an absolutely fabulous bathroom!"

It was a strange juxtaposition—the knotty-pine,
rocking-chair, kerosene-lamp, handmade-afghan main
room and the luxury-hotel-suite bathroom—a weird
combination Jane heartily approved of. In the back
of her mind there had been a dark fear that outhouses
might figure in this trip.

They got busy unpacking. This was a brief, casual
activity for Jane, but more like a well-planned mili-
tary maneuver for Shelley. There were outlets enough
in the bathroom for all of Shelley's various appliances and Jane's laptop, which she plugged in to
recharge. Their clothes, however, had to be hung in
a tiny alcove of the storeroom, with a burlap curtain
in place of a closet door.

"It smells fishy in here," Shelley complained.

"It's supposed to," Jane said. "If it didn't, they'd have to buy aerosol fish smell. It's a cabin in the woods. Back to nature and all that." She laughed. "Shelley, I have this vision of it being somebody's job to go around with plastic deer hooves on the end of a pole, making tracks outside the cabins when people are sleeping."

Shelley grinned. "On stilts!"

Once they'd made themselves at home, Jane said, "It's getting dark and I'm starving. Where do we eat?"

Shelley consulted the contents of the envelope she'd picked up at the main lodge. "Dinner tonight— uh-ho—in about fifteen minutes. We better get moving." She stepped out on the deck overlooking the woods. "It's getting cold, too. Bundle up and let's walk."

"Okay, but how will we find our way back? By Braille?"

"I've got flashlights," Shelley said complacently.

Jane rolled her eyes. "Of course you do." Even after years and years of being neighbors and best friends, Jane was still surprised frequently at Shelley's organizational skills. She was always prepared for almost anything. She probably had a first aid kit concealed somewhere on her person.

And a ham radio.

They put on their heavy coats and headed for the lodge. Jane was surprised at how brisk it was. The day had been unusually warm for fall, but as soon as the sun started going down, the thick forest seemed to extinguish the heat. And the sun went down very quickly indeed. In the five minutes it took them to reach the main lodge, it became almost entirely dark. As they approached the building, a creature scuttled across the road in front of them. "Oh, look! A raccoon!" Jane exclaimed, turning to Shelley, who had gone as pale as vanilla pudding.

"I don't like wild animals," Shelley said in a very small voice.

"Ah! A chink in the armor," Jane said with a laugh. "Just imagine them as school principals or bank managers or any of the people you regularly terrorize."

"Can't," Shelley said. "They have fur."

"Then imagine them bald," Jane said briskly.

Shelley shuddered. "A bald raccoon? Yuck!"

As they stepped onto the porch, Jane said, "Actually, that grocery store manager who didn't want to let you use expired coupons looked a bit raccoonish, and you didn't have a bit of trouble bullying him."

Jane pushed open the front door and they were enveloped in warmth, light, and the delicious odors of dinner. A fire crackled in a big central fireplace in the lobby, adding a hint of woodsmoke to the mix.

"Ah! You must be Mrs. Jeffry and Mrs. Nowack," a voice boomed. "I'm sorry we weren't here to greet you."

The speaker was a tall, lanky man who looked to be in his mid-fifties. He was wearing a red-and-black-checked flannel shirt, jeans, and suspenders with Santa Claus faces. He looked a bit Santaish himself, in spite of being thin. He had long, thick gray hair and a fluffy beard. "I'm Benson Titus. My wife, Allison, and I own the resort."

"Glad to meet you, Benson. I'm Jane and this is Shelley. This is a wonderful place," Jane said. "We were a bit surprised by the bathroom in our cabin."

He laughed, showing a spectacular mouthful of capped teeth, all of which were a bit too white. "We like our own comforts, Allison and I do, so we figured the guests would, too. Studied up on it and discovered that in most families, the wife picks the place to stay, and women tend to place a high value on good bathrooms. Cost the earth for all that fancy plumbing, but it did wonders for business."

"But isn't it going to be . . . well, sort of wasted on a bunch of high-school kids?" Shelley asked, mindful of their purpose in being there.

"Oh, the kids won't stay in those cabins. There are only ten of them and they're too remote to keep a close eye on. The kids will stay in the dorms. The cabins will be for the staff. I'll show you around the whole place in the morning. Dinner will be ready in about ten minutes, right through there," he added, pointing to large double French doors across the lobby. "Look around, make yourselves at home."

The dining room was enormous, with a high, wood-beamed ceiling and long, sturdy wooden picnic-type tables, laid with crisp blue-and-white-checkered oil-cloths. There were wooden benches with low backs rather than chairs. Another big fireplace was on the left wall, and the right and back walls, like the far wall in their cabin, were solid windows, with, they later discovered, a view over the lake and woods.

Only one table was set and occupied, that nearest the fireplace. A burly man with blond hair going to gray and in clothing that might have made him look like a lumberjack, had it not been so obviously newly purchased, was sitting at one end. The woman at the table was sitting as far from him as she could. She'd even turned away and had her legs stretched out to the fire. She was reading a battered paperback book, holding it very close to her face.

The man stood up as Jane and Shelley approached. "Well, I thought Marge and I were going to have to eat by ourselves. I'm John Claypool—Claypool Motors—and this is my brother Sam's wife, Marge. I usually call her Midge, 'cause she's such a cute little thing.''

Marge turned around, put down her book, and gave a weak smile that seemed to indicate that she'd heard this line several hundred times and never once enjoyed it.

"Marge and I know each other," Shelley said, then introduced herself and Jane. "Are we the only ones here?"

"My husband's on his way," Marge said. "He just had a couple business calls to make first. And two cars passed me on the road as I was walking down here." She had a very soft, sweet voice with the slightest hint of southern accent. She was a very pretty woman in an innocuous way. Blond-going-to-gray hair swept back from her face and held with old-fashioned hair clips, perfect, fair skin, very little makeup, and neutral-colored clothing—khaki slacks, white sweater and blouse, pale green scarf. Jane thought the one word that described her best was "clean." Or maybe "tidy." It was a toss-up.

Before anyone could launch a conversational gambit, another man entered the room and Marge went to meet him. "Sam, this is Shelley Nowack and her friend Jane Jeffry."

Unlike the rest of them, who were dressed for the outdoors, Sam Claypool had on dress slacks, a crisp white shirt, navy blue tie, and a blazer. If Jane hadn't known better, she'd have sworn he was an accountant, not a car dealer. He, too, was tidy—but too much so. His hair was a little too short, the creases in his slacks were perfect, his handshake was cool and impersonal. He needed rumpling, Jane thought. He'd come to dinner with a legal pad and hand-held calculator, which didn't strike Jane as especially sociable, even though she herself, like Marge, always had a paperback book somewhere on her person.

"Where's Eileen?" John asked.

Sam looked around. "I don't know. She was with me a minute ago." He had already sat down at the table and was punching in numbers on his calculator and making notes on the legal pad. Shelley was studying him ominously, as if considering giving a short lecture on social niceties.

Eileen Claypool, John's wife, turned up a moment later. "Sorry, dears, I had to take a potty break. The bathrooms here are amazing!" She was a perfect match for her husband—loud, oversized, and cheerful, like him. She had big blond hair, a huge, toothy smile, and was swathed about with an extraordinary number of accessories. Besides innumerable layers of clothing, she wore three necklaces, rings on every finger, a large purse, and two tote bags. "What a wonderful place this is. I'm Eileen. Who are you?"

Jane and Shelley introduced themselves again. Eileen proved to be a "hand holder," hanging on to them while the cloud of her expensive perfume encircled them. "Oh, you're those friends of Suzie Williams, aren't you?"

"Friends and neighbors," Shelley said, trying in vain to disengage her hand. "How do you know Suzie?"

"I've got a little dress shop. Just a hobby, really. Large sizes. I send a lot of my ladies to Suzie to get fitted for"—she lowered her voice to a muted bellow—"undergarments." Suzie, a big, gorgeous, vulgar platinum blonde whom Shelley and Jane were crazy about, was the head clerk of the lingerie section at the department store located in the neighborhood mall.

"Here, let's sit down. I want to know all about you ladies," Eileen said, dragging them over to the table. "Oh, Marge dear, I didn't even see you there. Got your books, I see. Marge always has her nose in a book," she explained. "Can't see how she does it. Reading puts me straight to sleep. Always has."

They were spared the full force of Eileen's attention by the arrival of yet another camper. "Oh, good, you haven't started eating yet! Hi, everybody. I'm Bob Rycraft. Mrs. Jeffry . . . Mrs. Nowack, how you doin'? I didn't know you'd be here. Mr. Claypool . . . Mr. Claypool, good to see you guys. I don't think I've met your wives."

While yet more introductions were conducted, Jane watched Bob move around the table. She didn't know him well, but had always liked him. He was a big, handsome, tawny man in his late thirties who moved with the lazy grace of a lion and had formerly been an athlete—football, Jane thought. Or maybe it was baseball. He and his wife and four little girls had moved to their suburb five years ago. Bob ran an apparently successful mail-order business that sold specialty paper products to companies all over the world. He was an extremely civic-minded guy, coaching at the YMCA and several schools, serving as Parks and Rec chairman on the city council and generously donating envelopes, packing boxes, and such to practically every good cause in town.

"So how are all those girls of yours?" Shelley asked him when they were all seated.

"Girls, girls, girls. I've got so darned many of them, I lose track," he said with a grin. "If we have any more, we're going to run out of names and have to start numbering them."

Shelley smiled back. Even though he was a man designed by nature to be father to mobs of rough-and-tumble boys, he was known to be besotted by his flock of dainty blond daughters.

"So who was the guy sneaking around outside?" Bob asked his table-mates.

"Sneaking?" Jane asked.

"Yeah, little scrawny guy. Was looking in the window and leaped away like a deer when he spotted me coming."

"Must of been Lucky Smith," Benson Titus said, coming from the kitchen with an enormous tray of food. He set out a platter of fried chicken, an enormous bowl of mashed potatoes, a giant pitcher of gravy, and two good-sized bowls of green beans on the table. "Start on this," he said, leaving to fetch another tray with the cornbread, butter, coleslaw, and a tossed salad. When he'd distributed the food, he sat down at an empty spot at the table. "Yeah, Lucky Smith is our local hunter thug who saw the light and turned environmental thug. He keeps a close eye on us here. But he's not dangerous, just a nuisance. Lucky grew up in these parts, a real good ol' boy, slaughtering everything he could hook or shoot.

"He got religion about the same time a group of enviro-Nazis started up in the county. Sorry. My wife says I shouldn't use that word, but sometimes it's the only one that fits. Anyhow, Lucky's decided it's his mission in life to keep an eye on the resort."

Shelley passed Jane the beans and whispered, "Trouble in paradise."

"Makes paradise more interesting," Jane replied.

Three

❖❖❖ "So what's this Lucky person do?" Marge Clay-
❖ pool said timidly, glancing around and seeming
to notice for the first time that two sides of the room
were windows with utter darkness beyond them.

"Nothing much," Benson said with a reassuring
smile. "He likes to gather a crowd and rant about
how he used to be a hunter and fisherman—I won't
spoil your dinner with any of the details—but he
came to his senses and God told him to devote his
life to returning nature to the indigenous residents."

"The Indians?" Jane asked.

"Oh, no. He says they came here from someplace
else, too. No, he means plants and animals. A real
Tree Hugger. But like most fanatics, he considers
himself the exception. He carries on about the tourist
trade bringing in all the people who wreck the land,
but he doesn't make any effort to remove his own
sorry carcass from the area."

Shelley had put down her fork. It was a dangerous sign,
when Shelley put down her silverware in the middle, let
alone the beginning, of a meal, Jane thought.

"You don't believe in saving the wildlife?" Shelley asked in a dangerously quiet voice.

Benson put up his hands as if to ward off an attack. "I surely do. That's why we left Chicago, because we love the wilderness. I've never shot a gun at any living thing. And I've never caught a fish that wasn't intended for eating. But I'm intolerant of fanatics."

Shelley picked her fork back up and nodded approval.

"Speaking of animals, there's really an enormous variety of them in the area," Benson said brightly, diverting the conversation. "In each of your cabins there are several handbooks. Mammals, fish, birds, and wildflowers, plus we have a little library next to the front desk where you can borrow books about geology, climate, natural resources, and history of the area. Please feel free to consult any of the books and take them to your cabins if you like. One of the things we're doing tomorrow is viewing a film about the natural history of this part of Wisconsin. Sounds dull, but I promise you'll enjoy it."

Jane noticed that Eileen Claypool had been dividing her attention almost equally between eating and watching Bob Rycraft eat. Understandable. Watching Bob Rycraft do anything was a pleasant activity. Now Eileen tore herself away from both activities to ask, "What else will we be doing tomorrow?"

"Anything you want," Benson said. "We've got lots of things planned, but you're all free to participate or skip them."

"We're here on behalf of the school board and the city council," Bob said. "I imagine we'll all want to participate." Then, apparently thinking that sounded too much like an order, he added, "Or won't we?"

There was a noncommittal murmur around the table.

"There's a real country breakfast in the morning," Benson said. "We go a little light on lunch, so you might want to stoke up in the morning anytime between eight and ten. At ten I'll give the official tour of the grounds and facilities. It would be a good idea for everybody to attend that."

"We certainly will," Shelley said. She made no bones about it being an order. Her tone had the precision and power of a dentist's drill. This time the murmur was of agreement.

Benson stared at her for a moment, collected himself, and went on. "We'll show the film at four in the afternoon. You can use the time after lunch for anything you'd like. Hiking around and exploring, relaxing and reading, or just taking a nap. Then tomorrow evening, we'll start some of the demonstrations of what we intend to provide. I'll be doing an outdoor cooking lesson at the main campfire area. All this is typed up with a more detailed map than you got when you checked in. I'll make sure you all have it before you leave the lodge tonight."

"Are we it? The whole group?" Sam Claypool asked. He'd been eating his dinner in a picky, preoccupied manner, as if his mind were miles away.

"No," Benson said. "A Mr. and Mrs. Flowers are coming. They called and said they'd had some car trouble, but should be here shortly. And the day after tomorrow the whole county's been invited to participate in classes if they want. That'll be the big day, with instructors and demonstrations. I've already got reservations for fifty for lunch, and there will be others—the ones who don't believe in reservations,'' he added with a broad smile.

"Liz Flowers?'' John Claypool asked. He'd shoveled down everything on his plate and was taking seconds. "Sold her a car once. Lady drives a hard bargain. Hope it's not that car that's broken down.''

"Liz is the president of the school board,'' Bob Rycraft explained to Benson. "I gotta warn you, she's expressed some doubts about this plan.''

Benson nodded. "I thought so. She was pretty cool on the phone.''

Jane realized for the first time that this was more than a vacation. She, like the rest of them, had a job to do. So far, she'd just accepted that a summer-school session here was a good idea. "What kind of doubts?'' she asked Bob.

"Oh, real practical things. Liability insurance, transportation costs, the availability of medical help because of the isolation,'' Bob said. "Important to consider, of course, but I'm sure it can all be worked out. The important thing is to get the kids out of their easy, comfortable suburban life for a while. Away from drugs, rap music, television, video games—all of that. I really believe you can do any child a world of good by bringing them back to nature—the *real* world—if only for a week or two. Gives them a sense of their own history, their place in the whole scheme—'' He broke off and grinned. "Sorry. I'm lecturing.''

"That's okay,'' Shelley said. "It's why we're

here. To share viewpoints, as well as learn about the facility."

"I think you've got something there," John Claypool said to Bob. "When Sam and I were kids, our folks sent us to camp for a couple summers and it was great!"

Sam, precise and tidy in his blazer, tie, and city-neat hair, just cocked an eyebrow.

John caught the look and said, "Yeah, I know you didn't like it as well as I did, but you were always a brainy kid, more interested in schoolwork than a good tussle with the boys."

"The 'boys' were savages," Sam said coldly.

Sam's wife, Marge, leaped in to avert controversy, as if by long habit. "This camp plan isn't just for boys, is it?" she asked too brightly.

Bob Rycraft answered. "We're hoping for two sessions. Either one for boys and one for girls, or possibly two mixed sessions—depending on a lot of factors."

"Like what?" Eileen Claypool said with a suggestion of a leer.

"Like the room arrangements," Bob said, apparently missing the leer. "You can't physically lock the kids up to keep the boys and girls apart. I'm sure there are fire regulations about that, and if there aren't, there should be. If the boys and the girls came at the same time, we'd have to pay for extra staff just to make sure they weren't sneaking out and meeting in the woods at night."

"On the other hand, how many of the girls are going to want to go camping if boys aren't involved?" Shelley asked.

Jane was on the point of echoing this sentiment when she realized she'd somehow slopped some gravy on her sleeve when she passed it to John Claypool. Since she'd brought a minimum of clothes, she thought she'd better wash it out. "Where's the rest room?" she said quietly to Benson, who was sitting at her end of the table.

"Next to the front desk," he replied.

She excused herself and went to wash out the cuff of her blouse. When she returned through the main lobby area, she noticed an older woman sitting by the fireplace. Wondering if this was Liz Flowers and not particularly eager to rejoin the group wrangling over sexual separation of teens, Jane approached the other woman and introduced herself.

"I'm Edna Titus, Benson's mother," the woman said. "You look chilled, Jane. Sit here with me for a minute."

"Gladly," Jane said, putting her hands out to the fire.

"Are you enjoying yourself?" Edna Titus asked.

"Oh, yes. But I'd underestimated my responsibility. I guess the word 'Wisconsin' has always meant 'vacation' to me. This is a lovely place."

"It is. We've been here about ten years, and I still wonder at the beauty. You're not a smoker, are you?"

"I'm afraid I am," Jane admitted. "I've been trying to stop for years and I can manage on about five cigarettes a day, but go berserk on any fewer."

"Oh, good! Somebody to be sinful with," Edna said. "This fireplace has such a nice draw that the smoke goes right up if you sit close enough."

She rose from her chair, sat on the raised flagstone hearth, and drew a battered pack of cigarettes from her sweater pocket. Jane studied her as Edna searched for a lighter. She was a tall, rangy woman who had probably never been pretty, but had an air of handsome dignity. Her gray hair was pulled into a casual knot on top of her head, her slacks and striped shirt were well worn and well kept. She was a woman who cared about her appearance, but not excessively so. She finally found her old-fashioned wick lighter, lit Jane's cigarette, then her own, and said, "So . . . ? What do you think?"

"Of what?"

"Of the chances the school board and city council will contract with Benson."

Jane felt instinctively this wasn't a person who could be tactfully lied to. "I have no idea. I really haven't been involved in the discussion until tonight. I assumed it was all but a done deal and we were just here to give a final approval, but now I'm not so sure."

Edna nodded. "Thanks for your honesty. Oh, it looks like our stragglers have arrived," she said as headlights swept across the front door. "I need to get their dinners ready. Would you mind greeting them?"

She hurried back to the kitchen. Jane put out her cigarette and went to the door. A tall, stately black woman with very short hair and a red, fringed poncho was coming across the parking lot with long, determined strides. She stepped onto the porch and took Jane's hand in an almost painfully firm grasp. "I'm Liz Flowers," she said. "You must be Jane

Jeffry. And this is my husband—'' She turned around and realized she was alone. ''Al? Have you lost yourself in the woods *already?* Where are you?''

''Just coming, hon.'' Al emerged from the darkness. He was taller and much darker skinned than Liz, and considerably heavier. Jane thought he looked like a Masai warrior who'd let his weight get out of hand.

''The owner's mother is warming up your dinner,'' Jane said. ''Come on inside.''

''See, Al? I told you that you wouldn't have to starve,'' Liz said. ''You didn't need to stop and get that packet of Oreos. Everyone else is here, I guess?'' she added to Jane, who was holding the door open. ''Thanks.''

Jane trailed along, bemused by the couple. Liz headed straight for the dining room without a moment's hesitation, as if she had an internal compass. She greeted those she knew, introduced herself to everyone else, told Al where to sit, and took Benson's now vacant place at the end of the table. Liz was forceful, energetic, and brisk.

Al Flowers appeared to be a mellow man happily caught in her force field. He gazed around the room, shaking his head slowly in approval. ''Nice place,'' he said, smiling vaguely.

''Well, of *course* it's nice,'' Liz said. ''We *knew* that from the brochures. Now, what's the plan?'' she demanded of the others. She hauled a large tote bag out from under her colorful poncho and plunged her hand into it. ''I've made some notes of things we need to look at, and propose that at least two people, working independently, evaluate each.''

"Now, Lizzie," Al said softly.

Amazingly, she stopped talking for a second, and stashed the notebook. "Okay, okay. But we have limited time and shouldn't be *wasting* it."

"There's plenty of time, Liz." He had a deep, rumbly voice.

Benson came through the kitchen doors with a tray of desserts just as Marge Claypool screamed.

Four

⟡ *"There was a face at the window!"*

Marge was white with fear and embarrassment at having made a scene.

"Must have been Lucky Smith," Benson said angrily. "I'm going to call the sheriff right now and see if Lucky can be watched more carefully. This is trespassing at the least and I won't have it!"

"No, no! Don't call the sheriff. Please," Marge said. "I don't want to make trouble for anyone."

"Marge is right," her husband, Sam, said. "It's late and we're all tired and we'd be up half the night if you call and get the sheriff out here."

Benson unwillingly agreed, but added, "He really is harmless. Obnoxious and distasteful, but harmless. I'm sorry he upset you, but don't let it spoil your dessert. It's my wife, Allison's, special recipe."

"Your wife?" Jane asked.

"Right. Allison's a little under the weather tonight and let the cook make dessert, but she'll be up and around tomorrow."

The dessert was divine—a shortcake that nearly

31

floated off the plate, crushed raspberries, and real clotted cream. Jane wasn't hungry after her big dinner, but she polished off dessert and barely restrained herself from licking the plate.

A couple of "Now, Lizzie's" from Al kept them from enduring an extra hour of planning sessions, which Lizzie dearly wanted to inflict on them, but it was still nearly ten o'clock when they started back to their cabins. Without anyone mentioning it openly, they agreed to move out in a group. Marge's fright had gotten under everyone's skin and made them all realize how far they were from their usual habitat.

"Benson and Allison," Jane said quietly to Shelley as they walked along the road, all four Claypools in a bunch in front of them, and the Flowerses following with Bob Rycraft. "I once dated a guy named Jan, but I refused to marry him because I didn't want to go through life as half of 'Jane and Jan.' "

"You're making that up," Shelley said.

"How'd you know?"

"Al, *will* you keep your flashlight pointed at the road?" Liz demanded. "You're going to trip and hurt yourself."

Jane and Shelley could barely hear the "Now, Lizzie."

When they were safely and comfortably locked up in their own cabin, Shelley declared first dibs on the fancy bathtub, and Jane bundled up to go sit on the back porch for a while. But she didn't last long. At first all she could hear was the pleasant burble of the now invisible stream running below and behind the cabin. But as her eyes and ears adjusted, she started imagining she could see tiny movements out of the

corner of her vision and hear scrabbling sounds in
the dried leaves. Probably just mice, she told herself.
Then she heard something much larger moving
around in the creek. Perhaps a big dog. Perhaps a
person.

She dragged a few logs inside and locked the
doors. She put them in the fireplace, but decided by
the time she got the fire going, they'd probably both
be asleep and she'd have to put it out again. Experience had taught her that this was a very smelly
process.

Shelley had just come out of the bathroom in her
robe with a towel around her head. "What's up?
You're not starting a fire this late, are you?"

"No. And what's up is spooky noises. Shelley,
does it strike you that the more often somebody says
someone else is harmless, the more alarmed you
become?"

" 'The lady doth protest too much'? Yes, I thought
if Benson said that one more time, I was going to
find the sheriff and throw myself on his manly
bosom. I'm sorry to say I'm already having bad feelings about this," Shelley admitted, fluffing her short,
dark hair with the towel.

"It got a lot better after the Flowerses arrived.
'Now, Lizzie,' " Jane added, doing a bad imitation
of Al's deep voice.

"Well, when there's a loony peering through the
windows, it's bound to make people nervous."

"Even before that," Jane said, pulling the drapes
that covered the glass wall overlooking the stream.
"Didn't you sense it? Or am I going a little batty?"

"Of course you're a little batty, but so am I. I

prefer to think of it as having 'enhanced sensitiv-
ity,' '' Shelley said. "Was it the Claypools who an-
noyed us? John and Eileen are so damned . . . hearty.
And Sam and Marge—well, she's shy and wimpy,
but he's almost antisocial. I'm suspicious of any man
who's too well groomed in the wrong circumstances.''

"He probably came straight from work,'' Jane
said. "We have to be fair.''

"Who says? Aren't we always telling our kids Life
Isn't Fair?''

"Kids! Yipes! I need to call and let them know I
got here. Otherwise my mother-in-law will be filing
the adoption papers in the morning.''

"She's staying at your house?''

"To my sorrow,'' Jane said. "She's probably already rearranged everything in my kitchen and gone
through my underwear drawer, sneering.''

"Well, call home and I'll start your bath running.
I brought along some fabulous bath salts I want you
to try.''

Jane looked at her friend warily. "Why didn't *you*
try them?''

Shelley just laughed. Maniacally, Jane thought.

Shelley woke early and puttered around quietly.
Jane was semiawake, but dozed off again until the
smell of coffee reached her. She staggered to the
bathroom, then poured herself some steaming coffee,
put her coat on over her robe, and went to sit on the
porch with Shelley. "Something tells me that when
my skin wakes up, I'm going to think it's cold out

here," Jane muttered, curling up in the rocking chair. "That sparkly stuff on the ground is frost, isn't it?"

"Uh-huh, but the sun is warming things up nicely already. You better knock that drink back pretty fast and get dressed or we'll miss breakfast."

Jane looked at her watch. "If I'm reading this right, it's five minutes until eight, and breakfast is from eight to ten."

"So—what's your point?"

Jane laughed. "Go on without me. I can hear your stomach growling."

It took Jane another leisurely hour to pull herself together. She got dressed, sent quick E-mails to Mel, her son, and her parents, and decided she wouldn't be using the laptop computer a lot on this trip, being as she had to sit in the bathroom doorway to use it since that was the only spot equidistant from the phone jack and the electrical plugs.

Walking down the road to the lodge, she felt silly about her uneasiness of the night before. How could she have thought there was anything ominous about a place so glorious? The sky was as blue as Paul Newman's eyes, and brilliant sunlight turned the autumn leaves to neon colors. The air was so clean and clear, it nearly shimmered. It was still nippy and she felt silly wearing a car coat, gloves, and a knitted hat, but wasn't about to freeze just to be fashionable.

The lodge was a different place this morning, too. Busy and much noisier than the night before. There were voices and the sound of dishes being stacked from the kitchen door, a radio playing a classical station at the front desk, the murmur of several conversations.

Marge Claypool, apparently recovered from her fright of the night before, was chatting with Benson's mother in front of the fireplace. Jane added her coat and hat to a pile of others on a sofa by the door and went into the dining room. Shelley and Liz Flowers had taken over a vacant table and had maps, charts, and books spread around. They were talking and both making notes on legal pads. *The Planners,* Jane thought. Shelley both loved and hated it when she found someone as well organized and bossy as she herself was.

Al Flowers was standing at one of the windows, hands behind his back, rocking back and forth slightly and humming something unidentifiable but cheerful. Bob Rycraft was wolfing down a huge breakfast. He was dressed in ratty gray sweats, and Jane guessed he'd already done some serious jogging.

Sam and John Claypool were eating at the same table. Sam looked slightly less businesslike today; he was wearing jeans, Jane noticed when he walked across the room to the buffet table. The jeans looked brand-new and still had store-bought creases down the legs, but at least he was trying.

Jane wandered over to study the buffet table just as a lanky teenaged boy brought out a fresh plate of pastries. The table was arranged with healthy foods at one end and delicious at the other. Jane glanced briefly at the sliced melons, granola bars, oat bran muffins, pitcher of skim milk, and a big bowl of something that looked like the revolting stuff her youngest son, Todd, fed his hamsters.

She passed it all by and concentrated on the bacon, eggs (scrambled or poached), biscuits and gravy,

pastries and butter, hash brown potatoes, grilled to-
matoes, and waffles with a choice of syrup, powdered
sugar, or honey to add a few necessary calories.

"Oh, thank God!" Eileen Claypool said. "I saw
all that stuff at the other end and thought I was con-
demned to starve. This is more like it."

"You and I seem to be the last ones to arrive,"
Jane said. "What are they going to do with everything that's left?"

"What makes you think I plan to leave anything?"
Eileen asked with a hearty laugh. "Sit with me, will
you? Those guys are talking about cars," she said,
glancing at her husband, brother-in-law, and Bob Rycraft. "Always cars. I get sick of hearing about them.
John always has two or three in the driveway that
he's trying out. Expects me to drive something different every day. Says it's good advertising."

Eileen wouldn't have been her first choice of dining companion, but Jane sat with her anyway. She'd
have preferred to hear about cars. She was still driving a ratty, rust-ridden station wagon that had hauled
around too many car pools. When her oldest son,
Mike, had graduated from high school the previous
spring, she'd bought him a snazzy black pickup truck
to take to college. Having gotten over the first shock
of the cost, she'd been giving an obsessive amount
of thought to getting a new vehicle for herself.

She was a great believer in making the necessary
sacrifices for her children, but had decided it might
not be strictly "necessary" for one of them to have
transportation *that* much better than her own.

The minute they, the last guests to eat, sat down,
the kitchen staff was allowed to eat. Two teenagers,

the resort owner, and a frail-looking woman Jane assumed was Benson's wife, Allison, came out from the kitchen. They all took a table near the doorway. Jane had held herself down to bacon, scrambled eggs, and a Danish. Eileen had piled her plate with some of everything fattening.

"So, Jane, tell me all about yourself," Eileen said through a mouthful of waffle.

"There's not much to tell," Jane said. *Not on demand, anyway,* she added mentally. "I'm widowed, have three kids. One each in college, high school, and junior high."

Eileen nodded, swallowed, and asked, "Are you from the Chicago area originally?"

"No, I'm not from anywhere. My parents are with the State Department, and until I was married, I'd never lived anywhere more than about six months. But my mother's people were from Illinois. And I've stayed in the same house almost all my adult life."

"Your parents still living?" Eileen slathered butter on a sweet roll.

"Yes, living and very active. They're in Finland right now."

Eileen sighed. "God, I wish I could say the same! Well, not about my parents. About John's. The farther away, the better. But it'll never happen."

"They're difficult?"

"Honey, 'difficult' is the mildest word you could use for them. They're horrible beyond imagining."

"In what way?" Jane asked. She wasn't really interested, but she was tired of being questioned and wanted to eat her breakfast.

"They're the stingiest people I've ever known.

Mean stingy and hateful to boot. I don't mean money, I mean they're stingy with compliments and everything. I tried to do up a little family history for John for his fortieth birthday and went to get information from them, and they flat out told me it was none of my business."

Eating and talking didn't seem to be difficult for Eileen to do at the same time. She was shoveling down her food. "They're both in frail health, live in a terrible house, and need lots of help. But they figure their boys have wives, and what are wives good for except taking care of them? That's why I opened the dress shop, to tell the truth. To have an excuse for not becoming their slave. Now when Mother Claypool calls and wants me to come over and clip her toenails or some damned thing, I can say that I can't leave the shop and I'll hire a new maid. Of course, she finds some excuse to fire her right away."

"What unpleasant people!" Jane said. "How old are they?"

"Both are in their eighties. Sam's the older brother, adopted actually, when they were already too old to be first-time parents. It was just like you hear about—many years of marriage without children, then when they adopted, Mother Claypool got pregnant with John. Do you know, this is the first time ever that all four of us have gotten away from them at once. Somebody always has to stay home to take care of them. Even Sam finally got tired of being their slave."

"Even Sam?" Jane asked, hoping the answer would allow her to finish her eggs.

"Oh, Sam's been the perfect son." Eileen said it

flatly, without a hint of sarcasm. "But even he's gotten a little snappish lately, which is weird because he's usually so cool and in control of everything. And Marge is a nervous wreck. You saw that last night. The parents are old and feeble and can't last forever—I hope. I know that sounds cruel, but I've never, in all these years, had a kind word from them. Oh, well, I didn't mean to chew your ear off about this."

Jane had managed to finish her breakfast.

She smiled and said, "No problem."

Five

❖❖ When everyone had finished breakfast, the tour
❖ of the camp commenced with the kitchens,
which were much larger than Jane would have
guessed. Given enough staff, a great many people
could be fed at once. And there was plenty of room
for staff to live along the corridor leading off the
kitchen area. Benson explained that, as with most
summer resorts, the bulk of the employees were college students.

"It's harder to find a reliable supply of workers
during the school year, but we manage," he said.
"We usually close the Conference Center and just
cater to small groups that occupy the cabins."

"What about our own teachers we'd bring along?"
Liz Flowers asked briskly.

"They could stay in the cabins, provided reservations are made well in advance, but you'd probably
want them in the Conference Center with the students," Benson replied. "And there would be an
extra charge, I'm afraid."

"Oh, yes. They'd definitely want to be with the

kids in the Conference Center!'' Bob Rycraft said enthusiastically.

Shelley muttered to Jane, ''Handsome, but dim. Why would any sane adult *want* to be locked up with a bunch of teenagers day and night? I had a great-aunt who decided to spend her sunset years as a housemother in a boarding school. She lasted one semester and needed years of psychiatric care to get over it. She tended to drool, and become startled at sudden noises.''

''I guess there are people like us who manage, sometimes with considerable effort, to love our own teenagers, and then there are those rare and misguided individuals who love all of them,'' Jane said, shaking her head. ''He appears to be one of those. Just wait until all those little girls of his hit puberty about the same time.''

''People like him must have suffered either a great deal more or a lot less of the usual angst when they were teens, I suppose,'' Shelley said. ''I can hardly think about those years without shuddering.''

''Ladies?'' Liz said sharply.

They hurried along to catch up with the group. They exited from the back door of the staff wing, turned right, and walked down a long, winding incline at the bottom of which was a spectacularly beautiful lake. It was fronted by a beach of sorts— not sand, but shingle. A small dock had a single elderly rowboat tied up, and there was a large swimming dock farther out. A shed contained a great many neon orange life jackets, and an old-fashioned wooden lifeguard tower stood sentry. A list of commonsense rules was posted on the front of the tower.

It was cool enough that the thought of swimming made Jane shiver, but in the summer it would be a different matter.

"We're lucky that there's a very slow, gentle slope here," Benson was saying. "And over there, the roped-off area is only four feet deep. That's where we give beginner swimming lessons. Oh, I almost forgot to mention poison ivy."

"There's poison ivy here?" Marge asked.

"There shouldn't be," Benson said with a smile. "I've conducted a war against it ever since we arrived. I don't think there's any left, but I have a handout with drawings and photos of it for you. If anybody sees so much as a leaf of it, please let me know."

Jane glanced around at the group. Liz, naturally, had a clipboard and was taking notes like mad. She even had a tape measure and marked down the height of the lifeguard tower. Bob Rycraft had gone down to the shoreline and was smiling and nodding, no doubt picturing the lake full of happy kids who would go home and say no to drugs and study like mad, all because of two glorious weeks at camp. Al Flowers had wandered over to the tower and, hands in pockets, was looking up as if contemplating someone other than himself climbing it.

The Claypool brothers were standing together, talking quietly, probably about cars, not camp, Jane guessed. John, the big, blond, beefy younger brother, had his hands clasped behind his back and was looking down, nudging a rock around with his toe. It was a curiously subservient pose for the bigger, brasher man to take.

Meanwhile, Sam's wife, Marge Claypool, was glancing uneasily at the dense woods, looking very nervous, and John's wife, Eileen, had found a log to sit on. She'd taken off her shoe and was massaging her foot.

Benson, apparently realizing that he was being largely ignored, stopped explaining the lake and safety regulations and left them to their own thoughts for a few minutes before saying, "Okay, let's go back up the hill and look at the Convention Center."

Eileen Claypool grunted slightly as she laboriously leaned forward to put her shoe back on and gather up all her loose belongings. Even for this tour, she was loaded up with jewelry and tote bags.

The Convention Center turned out to be a large, plain building to the north of the main lodge. It was clearly newer than the rest of the camp: two stories, white clapboard and faintly naked-looking. Though neat and freshly painted, it had no shutters, no foundation plantings, almost no ornamentation at all.

"A bit of an abomination, isn't it?" Shelley said under her breath.

"It certainly doesn't fit in very well," Jane responded. "Sort of like a habited nun at a cocktail party."

"Yes!" Shelley said. "The kind of habit with the big white winged headgear."

Either Benson or the architect had attempted to make the big building look friendlier by adding a porch outside the front door. But it was little, flimsy, out of proportion, and looked as if it had blown up against the building and was merely resting there for a moment before moving on about its business.

The inside of the Convention Center was much like the outside: plain, clean, practical, and aggressively boring. The ground floor contained a dining area with a practical, spotlessly clean expanse of blue linoleum flooring, white Formica tables, and folding chairs with blue seats that just missed matching the floor and consequently made both look shabby. The rest of the area was for exhibits and meetings. There was sturdy carpet here and lots of room dividers.

Overall, Jane found it terribly bland and depressing, especially in contrast to the cozy cabin she and Shelley were sharing. But the kids wouldn't care. They'd be outdoors most of the time and more interested in each other than the building. If kids cared about their surroundings, she reasoned, their own bedrooms at home wouldn't look quite so much like the aftermath of a nuclear holocaust.

Benson led them downstairs, where there were locked storage bins that looked like little jails and a very large room with a whole fleet of room dividers on wheels. Benson explained that the dividers were specially designed to provide soundproofing, so many small meeting rooms could be constructed by just sliding them around.

Next they went from a center staircase to the second-floor dormitory area. A long, single hallway stretched both ways. He opened a couple doors along it to let them look at the rooms, which were sparse but neat. Each had a single bathroom with a shower stall, a big window that looked out over the woods, either two or three single beds in various arrangements, a functional, indestructible desk, and several chairs. It looked like one of the dormitories of Jane's youth, and she found herself wondering how any adult could survive staying in someplace so essentially "institutional" without going screaming mad.

Shelley was watching her reaction. "Bad vibes?" she asked.

"Very bad," Jane admitted. "And I don't know why. I think I must have been in a mental institute that looked just like this in a previous life."

Shelley nodded. "Or a sanatorium where frail Victorian ladies went to die of tuberculosis. Still, I don't think the kids would care. And when they get their own 'stuff' in here, it'll look more cluttered, if not better."

When they came back out into the hallway, the rest of the group was milling around, seemingly as anxious to get away as Shelley and Jane were—all, that is, except Liz, armed with clipboard and asking Benson about heating and cooling, elevator-inspection schedules, handicapped access and fire regulations and all the practical considerations Jane never would have thought of.

Al Flowers was standing next to them, leaning against the wall and watching his wife. "Isn't she a wonder?" he said admiringly.

He was just what Jane needed at that moment. A big, gooey jolt of contentment. A man who was proud of his wife. "You're a good man, Al Flowers!" she said with a smile.

They gathered up Bob Rycraft, who seemed determined to enthusiastically examine every room, and left the building. "Now we're in for a bit of a walk," Benson warned them cheerfully, "but it'll be worth it."

"I'll bet," Eileen Claypool muttered. She had developed a serious limp.

The group returned to the main lodge, circled it, and continued south along the road that ran past their cabins. Benson took it slow and easy, allowing them to stop in their cabins and get cameras (Liz and Shelley), binoculars (Marge), Band-Aids (Eileen), and take bathroom breaks (Jane). Just beyond the cabins, the road turned into more of a path and rose slightly.

"Look at Marge," Shelley whispered.

Jane glanced back. Marge was walking extremely close to Sam, surveying the woods around them with quick glances. "She doesn't like nature much, does she?" Jane whispered back. "I guess the outdoors just isn't for everyone."

"She's been jumpy the whole time we've been around her," Shelley said. "It's odd. I don't know her well, but I've been on lots of committees with her. She's always seemed shy and retiring, but more placid than nervous."

"Well, there *was* that face she saw at the window."

Shelley shook her head. "No, I noticed it before she had her screaming fit. It's like she was already scared of something. Or somebody."

Jane looked at Shelley sharply for a moment, then laughed. "You've let the dreary atmosphere of the Conference Center get to you. Next thing you'll be wanting to stay up late with the lights off and tell ghost stories. And maybe drop aspirin in your soft drink to get drunk."

The next stop in the tour of the grounds was much more pleasant. It was one of three campfire sites.

"We believe that preparing and eating food outdoors can be enjoyable," Benson said as they came up the last small rise. "It doesn't have to be hot dogs and hamburgers and potato chips. It's possible to cook a really fine meal over a campfire. This is where we'll be eating dinner tonight, and I'll be demonstrating some outdoor cooking techniques you might enjoy."

It was a nicely mowed area encircling a large campfire site. A low wall of fieldstone defined the fire area, which was already stacked with logs and ready to be lighted. There were a few well-tended chrysanthemums blooming around the nearer side of the grassy verge.

"Oh, Jane!" Shelley said, grabbing her arm. "Look at that view!"

Turning around, Jane realized the woods had been skillfully cleared to offer a view out over the cabins and the lake beyond. She also couldn't help noticing that the sky was clouding up and there was a chilly wind. "Eating dinner here might be a nippy proposition," she said.

"I don't suppose you brought long underwear?" Shelley asked.

"I don't *own* long underwear, Shelley. I live in a house, not a tent."

"Never mind. I brought extra," Shelley said.

"Of course you did," Jane said. "You're always prepared for anything. But Liz has a tape measure along. That puts her a point ahead of you."

Shelley looked at her, slitty-eyed. "Wanna bet?"

Liz was asking Benson about medical services.

"The closest fire station," he said, "was just beyond the road where you came in. Before you crossed the bridge. They have an ambulance. The county hospital is five miles from here. We'll have a nurse on duty who can treat minor injuries.''

"Poor Benson," Jane said. "I'll bet he didn't expect to be grilled quite so thoroughly."

"But he's got all the answers," Shelley pointed out. "He's obviously done his homework."

"He does seem awfully eager to impress us, doesn't he?" Jane said.

"For all his scruffy looks, he's a businessman, and that Conference Center must have cost a fortune," Shelley replied. "He might have overestimated the number of people who would want to use it. This school thing would bring in a lot of m—"

Just then Marge screamed again.

Six

❖ "Sorry, ma'am, didn't mean to scare you," the
newcomer said.

He was a tall, dark man in his fifties with alarm-
ingly heavy eyebrows. He'd come, silently, by some
other route than the rest of the group and had taken
them all by surprise, though only Marge had such a
violent reaction. He was dressed all in khaki, including his Smoky the Bear hat.

"Sheriff Taylor, ma'am," he said.

"Not Sheriff Andy Taylor by chance," Jane asked
with a chuckle.

He looked at her wearily. "No, ma'am. And I
don't have a deputy named Barney Fife, if you were
going to ask."

"Nothing like pissing off the law," Shelley
murmured.

"Guess he's heard that little jest before," Jane
grumbled.

Marge still had her hand over her mouth. She lowered it and said, "I'm so sorry. You just seemed
to . . . appear out of nowhere!"

He nodded at her and turned to Benson. "I got your message this morning about your prowler, and Allison said you were out here. Since it was on my way home, I thought I'd just stop by. Whoever it was, it wasn't Lucky Smith. I had him in the lockup on a drunk-and-disorderly. Who was it who saw the prowler?"

Benson introduced Marge. Sheriff Taylor took this in an even more world-weary manner. He was obviously thinking, *Of course it was the screamer.* But he merely said, "Oh, well. Okay, ma'am, what did this person you saw look like?"

"Just li—just a face. It was only for a second."

"White? Black? Young? Old?"

"White. I couldn't guess the age."

"A man?"

"Oh, yes. Look—I'm sorry for causing you trouble. It's nothing. Really," Marge said, wilting under his eyebrow-hooded glare.

Her husband, Sam, was merely observing, as if he had no connection with her. Jane thought how pleasant it would be to slap him.

"Just everybody use caution, will you?" Sheriff Taylor said it as if he were speaking to a group of slow-witted kindergartners. He gave Benson a half wave, half salute and disappeared as silently as he'd arrived. He hadn't actually used the words "hysterical" or "menopausal," but they seemed to hover in the air like gnats.

Benson said, with awesome good cheer, "Okay, we've done the basic tour." He glanced at his watch. "There will be soup and sandwiches served in about an hour. You're free to do whatever you want for now. And after lunch, we'll begin our programs. As I think I told you last night, I put a notice up at the courthouse and in the county paper for the local people who want to attend, too. Free entertainment is pretty sparse around these parts, and a long winter is looming. Oh, and my wife has literature for you at the lodge. More detailed maps, some suggestions we're making for classes and activities for your school, and such. Stop by and pick them up at your convenience.''

Jane caught up with Marge, who was leaving as quickly as she could. "Don't pay any attention. That's a lout of a man," she told the other woman, who looked perilously near tears. Jane prided herself on *not* saying, *And so's your husband.*

"I know. Thanks. It's just that there have been strange things lately.''

"What kind of strange things?'' Jane asked.

Marge reclasped her barrette to capture a fine piece of fair hair. "Oh, nothing. Sam says it's my imagination. It probably is. I wonder what we'll have for dinner,'' she inquired, changing the subject so brutally that even Jane couldn't twist it back.

They had the dubious honor of meeting Lucky Smith when they got back to the lodge. He was sitting on the porch as if he belonged there. He was a stringy, weasely old man—or maybe he wasn't so old, but had just lived too hard. His hair was thinning, dyed, and greasy, his eyes small and red. And in the center of his rather pinched face was a nose big and red enough to belong to a much larger man. Shelley started giggling when she saw him.

"Imagine what he looked like as a baby," she said. "What a cute new nose—er, baby you have, Mrs. Smith."

But her smile faded as Lucky Smith staggered to his feet, pointed at Benson Titus, and said in what he no doubt thought was the Voice of Doom, "Hear you been makin' false accusations against me, Titus."

"Oh, Lucky, give it a rest. I'm busy," Benson said. "Go home and finish sobering up. Now, Mrs. Flowers, I'll get those files you wanted to see," he added, trying to steer Liz and the rest of the group away from Lucky.

"Busy with the Devil's work!" Lucky shouted. "Ruining God's world. The Devil's man, that's what you are, Titus. You have to meet your Maker at the Pearly Gates, and God himself is gonna say, 'Why'd you cut down my trees to build that big ol' building just to line your pockets with gold? Those were My trees, Titus.' That's what God's gonna say to you. And then what good is all your gold gonna do you?"

Shelley was no longer laughing. "That's a real loony," she said once they were inside the lodge with the door firmly shut behind them.

Benson heard her. "He's only this bad when he's coming off a drunk." He was trying to be reassuring, but it was obvious he was very upset. He went straight to the phone. Jane and Shelley went to sit by the fireplace and could hear Benson saying furiously, "Tell Taylor to send somebody out here right now to get this maniac off my property. He's harassing my guests. I won't have any more of this. If he turns up here again, I'm going to file a lawsuit against the county that'll knock your socks off. I have the right to be protected from this lunatic!''

"Can't say I blame him," Shelley said quietly.

Jane inched closer to the fire. She hadn't realized how chilly she really was until she felt the warmth. "Imagine having to cope with someone like that!"

A few minutes later, a patrol car arrived. Through the front windows they could see a man in uniform approach Lucky and start talking to him. Lucky kept gesturing and shouting, but the officer kept his cool, nodding and continuing to talk. Finally Lucky calmed down and was led away to the car and off the property.

Jane and Shelley settled in to watch others who were coming in. A dozen or so people who seemed to be acquainted passed through to the dining room. Jane supposed they were local people who had decided to make a little mini vacation by staying overnight before the next day's activities. Several young people, presumably students, headed for the kitchen, and one professorial-looking older gentleman arrived with a slide projector, screen, and briefcase. Edna Titus came down the stairs behind the front desk and greeted him.

"Who's that?" Shelley asked.

"Benson's mother. I had a chat and a smoke with her out here last night."

Edna approached them and was introduced. "You haven't seen my sweater, have you, Jane?"

"I have. Where? Oh, on one of the rockers on the porch."

Edna went off to fetch her sweater, and Jane and Shelley went into the dining room. Their idea of a "light lunch" was an apple and a piece of cheese. Benson's was a selection of four different kinds of sandwiches, three soups, an assortment of chips, dips, nuts, cheeses, soft drinks, coffee, fancy tea bags, another platter of melon—in balls this time instead of slices—and two salads.

"I'm going to go home weighing four hundred pounds," Shelley said. "I'll have to wrap up in a tent because my clothes won't fit."

"Nonsense. We're burning off every single calorie just by walking around in the cold," Jane said. "Now, dig in."

Jane felt so stupefied by lunch that she couldn't face a lecture. If she were to sit quietly, she knew it would be only moments before she was sound asleep and snoring repulsively.

"I know I should be taking my responsibilities more seriously," she told Shelley, "but I'm going to go take a nap."

Shelley flapped a hand dismissively. "Go ahead. We don't actually need to know about the wildlife in order to make an intelligent recommendation on sending the kids here. Unless, of course, they're going to tell us about something huge and vicious that eats teenagers."

"If so, ask if they're for sale," Jane said.

As Jane sluggishly made her way back to their cabin, she realized it was misting and there was a faint, faraway rumble of thunder. A perfect afternoon for a nap. She made a quick E-mail run on the computer, picking up a delightfully personal note from Mel, a plea from her daughter, Katie, that Jane autho-

rize Grandma to advance funds for a shopping trip—
funds Jane would reimburse, of course—and a note
from her son Mike asking her opinion of his joining
the college band, which would require the purchase
of a tux.

She replied to all of the notes briefly.

"Me, too," to Mel.

"No," to Katie.

And "Let me think about it," to Mike.

She sent the notes off, removed her shoes, and
snuggled into bed for a nice, cozy snooze.

When Jane woke, she thought she'd overslept and
it was night. But it was merely overcast and had
apparently rained quite hard while she was napping.
Not nice for a camp-out. She was still stumbling
around trying to get her bearings when Shelley came
in wearing an oversized khaki poncho with a hood.

"Ah, the tent wardrobe already!" Jane said.

"If it isn't Sleeping Beauty." Shelley exclaimed.
"And I'll have you know I haven't eaten a bite since
lunch." She bent way over and let the poncho slide
off over her head. "I brought you one of these, too.
They're really toasty. Flannel-lined and everything.
Benson loaned us a bunch."

"What can you possibly imagine I'd need it for?"
Jane asked.

"Why, to wear to the campfire dinner, of course."

"Shelley, you're kidding! What do I look like?
Admiral Byrd? Noah? An idiot? It's cold and rainy
out there."

"No, it's not so bad. The rain's stopped and it's

actually a little warmer now than it was earlier. It'll be fun.''

"Compared to what? Having our fingernails ripped out?''

"What a poop you're being,'' Shelley said. "A *poop,* I say! Come on. You'll see I'm right. If you really, really hate it, you can come back here and starve. This is dinner we're talking about, Jane.''

"You mean we don't get to eat unless we go sit in the rain?''

"First, it's not really raining—''

Jane gestured at the glass doors. "Shelley, that silvery wet stuff falling out there is rain.''

"No, it's just the residue of rain dripping off the leaves,'' Shelley said sweetly.

"Oh, of course. That makes a huge difference.''

"And secondly, you can stay here and eat if you want. I think there are some of those neon orange crackers with peanut butter in my car. At least, they were there last summer. They might be a little smashed, but they'll taste the same as ever. And I'm pretty sure there's some room-temperature ginger ale somewhere in my luggage. What a feast!''

"How do you get into these tent garments?'' Jane asked with a sigh.

Seven

❖❖ Once she had donned the long underwear,
❖ extra socks, and the lined poncho, Jane had to
admit—not out loud to Shelley, of course—that she
was quite comfortable. And the rain had stopped,
though there were still flashes of lightning in the
western sky and occasional low murmurs of thunder.
As she and Shelley headed up the road to the campsite, they could see Liz and Al Flowers's tall forms
ahead of them and could hear John and Eileen Claypool's loud voices behind them.

The campsite had been transformed. Instead of a
bland, green area with a circle of rocks, it was full
of people and color. There was a large, rather spread-
out, glowing fire inside the ring of rocks, which had
burned down to orange embers. Various cooking gad-
gets surrounded it.

There was a table set up for food preparation to
one side of the campfire and a canopy-style tent covering a long table and benches on the other side.
Benson was too busy to do much more than call out
greetings as they gathered. His mother, his wife, and

two young men were acting as helpers. Bob Rycraft must have been the first arrival and was getting in everyone's way. Jane could imagine Bob taking his enthusiasm home and digging a fire pit in his backyard. In his khaki poncho, he looked even more like a sleek, contented lion curiously exploring.

Jane was feeling enthusiastic herself. The smell was divine: a mix of pines, woodsmoke, rain, and food. Better than any perfume.

Jane and Shelley joined Al Flowers at the table. Liz, naturally, had gone to the preparation table and was no doubt driving poor Benson mad with questions. The table was laid with a flowered tablecloth with matching napkins, and while their plates were heavy plastic, the silverware was real. "What a transformation!" Shelley said to Al.

He rumbled amiable agreement.

Eileen and John Claypool joined them. Eileen was so bundled up under her poncho that she waddled. She had on one boot, and on the other foot, a fuzzy pink house slipper with a plastic bag tied around it. "Does this place ever smell great!" she said. "What are those metal boxes around the fire?"

"Reflector ovens," Al said. "There's a cake in one of them." His sparkling white grin against his dark face and the dark background of pines made Jane think of the Cheshire cat.

She turned a little so she could catch some light from the fire on her watch. It was only six o'clock, but it could have been midnight—or four in the morning. If you were out here without a clock and knew nothing of stars, how would you tell what time it was? she wondered. To a city person, the complete darkness was eerie. At home, dark meant no sun, but streetlights, car headlights, and the perpetual glow of Chicago filling the southern sky. Here, on a cloudy night, darkness was complete and primitive and over-whelming. It was both peaceful and frightening a combination she wouldn't have believed could exist at the same time.

Sam and Marge Claypool were the last to arrive. They were clad in matching blue raincoats with hoods. Sam looked embarrassed, perhaps at being dressed like his wife, and they both looked cold and forlorn. Marge was a bundle of nerves. She immediately joined the group at the table and sat so she was facing the woods, rather than having them at her back. Sam went and stood by the fire with his thin, long-fingered hands outstretched to it.

"I don't think that woman looks well," Eileen said in a surprisingly quiet voice to Jane.

"What woman?"

"Mrs. Titus. The younger one. Benson's wife."

Jane shifted a bit so she could look at Allison. She'd only seen her once before and hadn't really paid much attention, but Eileen was right. Allison Titus was a small, frail woman and looked very pale and ill. Her movements were slow and vaguely de-feated. As Jane stared, Allison, who was dicing up some vegetables, paused for a moment and put her hand to her heart. Then she scooped up the vegeta-bles, put them in a pot, and picked up the pot to carry to the fire. Instantly her mother-in-law, Edna Titus, was at her side, apparently chiding her. Allison sighed, put the pot back down, and Edna took it to the edge of the fire and set it on a metal grill that sat above the embers.

The small scene was over in seconds, but was telling. "How nice it must be," Jane said to Eileen, "to have a mother-in-law so concerned for your welfare."

"You're telling me! Is yours a bitch, too?"

"Not as demanding as yours, but Thelma's a pretty tough cookie. She just didn't think anybody, least of all me, was good enough to marry her oldest son. But then her younger son married someone she considered even more unsuitable, and that took some of the heat off me."

"Must have been nice, married to the favorite son," Eileen groused.

"Okay, folks," Benson said, coming to the table. "We'll be ready to eat in a few minutes. Everything's almost ready."

"What are we having?" John Claypool asked eagerly.

"A feast!" Benson replied. "I buried a big, lean brisket in the coals this afternoon. The boys are digging it out now. While they're slicing it, I'll do some fish in one of the reflector ovens since the fish only takes a few minutes. The vegetable mix is steaming in that pot on the grill right now, and my mother is doing battered apple rings in the big fry pan. If this were summer, we'd be serving a big salad of native greens, but unfortunately it's too late in the season. There are twice-baked potatoes in a couple of pots that are buried in the coals."

"Excuse me while I drool!" Eileen said.

They all listened like obedient students while Benson "introduced" them to the equipment, ingredients, and methods of cooking he'd employed. Different foods were cooked at different temperatures, which meant different distances from the heat source. It was necessary to learn to skillfully manage long-handled forks, spoons, and knives, he said. Jane was astonished that he made it sound like fun. Well, it might be, if you had all the help he had.

When the dinner was finally served up, Jane decided it was probably the very best meal she'd ever eaten in her life. The brisket was so tender, it broke apart with a fork. It had been marinated in a tangy sauce, a couple of homemade, unlabeled bottles of which were set out on the table. There was a spicy cheese sauce over the steamed vegetables, and the baked, crumb-covered fish was thin, crisp outside, moist inside, and utterly delicious. She tried to eat slowly and savor it all, but found herself packing it in like a starving lumberjack and couldn't help wondering if there was any way to conceal a few more of the fried apple rings somewhere about her person for snacking on later.

Liz even stopped her inquisition to eat. Benson's wife and mother sat down with the guests at the big table while Benson and the young helpers kept bringing more food. Edna had a healthy appetite, but Allison just picked. Jane wished she knew the woman well enough to suggest that she looked like death warmed over and should be home in bed. Instead, she said, "This is a wonderful meal! Surely you don't eat this well here all the time."

Allison smiled and suddenly looked much younger and healthier. "As a matter of fact, we do, most of the time. The county junior college offers a culinary degree as part of their hotel management course. We usually have an intern here, getting credit hours for practical experience. We don't have to pay them much, but the grocery bills are pretty high sometimes. Every once in a while we get one who would like to specialize in seafood preparation, which can be pretty expensive. I like it best when we have a pastry enthusiast.''

Jane gasped and turned to Shelley. "Do we have a cooking school anywhere near us?''

Allison laughed. "You didn't when we lived there.''

"You lived near us?''

"Yes. That's why we thought of contacting your city council and school board instead of someone else. I noticed your address and Mrs. Nowack's when you signed in. Your street backs up to that vacant field, doesn't it? Is it still vacant?''

"Yes. And my cats love it that way. I think they'd buy the land if they had any money.''

"We were supposed to have a new house built there," Allison said. "Then the builder got in trouble and went bankrupt, as you know. That's when we decided to move up here. We'd already sold the house we lived in and we'd been visiting this resort for years. On a whim, Benson called the owner and asked if there was any chance he'd sell. To our astonishment, he was not only willing, but eager. So here we are.''

"It's a beautiful area," Jane said. "But it's awfully remote. Don't you get lonely?''

"Never," Allison said emphatically. "For one

thing, there are guests here about nine months out of
the year, and I've met some fascinating people. And
the rest of the time, Edna and Benson are the best
companions a person could want. I have lots of proj-
ects, too. I make quilts and afghans and we've got a
satellite dish, so there are always movies to watch
on television. And I've got a computer and corre-
spond with quilters and resort owners all over the
world.''

This led to a discussion of E-mail, usenets, the
World Wide Web, and a promise to get together the
next day so that Allison could show Jane some nifty
places to visit via computer and modem and check
out the irritating error message Jane got on her laptop
occasionally. A half hour earlier, Jane had been pity-
ing Allison. Now she was very nearly jealous of her.
What a full, satisfying life Allison Titus lived out in
the wilds.

''Is anybody but me an unrepentant smoker?'' Al
asked the group when they'd finished eating.

Jane and Edna admitted as much and walked down
to the road to indulge themselves well away from
Bob Rycraft's more-in-pity-than-in-anger gaze. Al
brought along a tin can with a half inch of water in
it to serve as an ashtray. They found a log to sit on
and Edna said, ''Al, what do you do for a living?''

''I work for a bank,'' he said.

''Oh? I used to work at a bank as a teller when I
was young. What do you do there?''

''I'm the president,'' he said with a grin.

Edna and Jane simultaneously yelped with
laughter.

Al looked embarrassed. "Well, it's a really small bank."

They smoked in companionable silence for a few minutes, then returned to the group just as Benson was unveiling a pineapple-upside-down cake that had been cooking in one of the reflector ovens. Almost everyone protested that they were too full to eat any more; well, maybe just a bite or two. The cake disappeared at an alarming rate.

"What a lot of stuff you've got to carry back," Jane said to Benson.

"We'll just take back the food tonight. The boys will come back for all the cooking utensils in the morning. They're too hot to carry around now," he said with a satisfied grin. His party had been a great success.

The young men, who had already packed up most of the leftover food, now dragged out a banjo and a guitar and prepared to entertain them. They played a couple folk-song-sounding numbers that Jane didn't recognize, but liked, and then began to play "Bridge Over Troubled Waters."

To nearly everyone's astonishment, Sam Claypool started singing with them. He had an amazingly good voice. The young men kept playing and quit singing in honor of the superior performer. When the last note died away, they were all silent for a long moment, then John started clapping. "Still got the talent, haven't you, Sam? Good job!"

Everybody else joined in the applause. Sam actually smiled, and Jane realized he was quite a good-looking man. It was a shame his smile was so infrequent. Everyone urged him into singing some more, and after consultation with the young men with the instruments, he obliged. He sang another folk song and then one of Jane's favorites, "Love Hurts," which always reduced her to tears. Jane was surprised that a man who appeared to have so little personality and social grace could put so much feeling into a song.

The concert was cut short by a crack of thunder and a sudden, short burst of rain. The campfire hissed and steamed. The young men put their instruments back in their protective cases. Edna and Allison started gathering up silverware and linens. Jane and Shelley tried to help, but were shooed away.

"You're our guests. We don't let guests help," Edna said firmly. "Scoot on back to your cabins before you get drenched."

"The rain's already stopping," Jane protested, but to no avail. She and Shelley got their flashlights and picked their way down the short incline to the road. Eileen was somewhere behind them, fretting about her pink slipper getting wet. Liz was advising her on the proper care of blisters.

The cabin was warm and cozy. They got out of their ponchos and the top couple layers of their clothing. Jane went to pull the drapes and realized that it had stopped raining and there was moonlight filtering down through the trees. "What bizarre weather," she said.

"That was one of the best meals and nicest evenings I can remember. Want a cup of coffee?"

"I don't suppose you have tea, do you?" Jane asked. She lighted the fire she'd prepared and abandoned the night before. The kindling crackled, spit, belched smoke, and suddenly burst into tiny flames that licked hungrily at the bark on the logs.

"I have tea bags and one of those little coil heaters," Shelley said.

"I'm surprised you didn't bring a cappuccino machine along."

They fixed their drinks and sipped them in friendly silence. Jane sat on the floor in front of the fireplace, marveling at what a nice little fire she'd managed to create and feeling hypnotized by the sight, sound, and smell of it.

"I think I may just sleep in my clothes," Jane finally said. "I'm too tired to get up and take them off."

"We might as well go to bed early, I guess," Shelley said. "What time is it?"

Jane glanced at her watch—or rather, her bare wrist. "Shelley, my watch is gone."

"It's probably in your purse. Or on the bathroom counter."

"No, I looked at it when we got to the campsite. Oh, rats! I've lost my watch!"

"We'll go look for it in the morning."

"After it rains all night? Can't you hear the rain starting up again?"

Shelley groaned. "It's not waterproof?"

"I think so, but it could get washed away or covered with mud and I'll never find it." She was donning her sweater. "The kids got it for my birthday. I can't lose it."

"You're not going out alone," Shelley declared. She was shaking the moisture off her poncho.

It was raining in earnest by the time they slogged

their way back to the campsite, which was now deserted. The fire was out, the cooking utensils were stacked together, getting a bath in the rain. The formerly festive table was naked, and its tentlike canopy had been dismantled and taken away. Jane and Shelley minced around, shining their flashlights at the ground, hoping to catch a glint of the missing watch.

"I don't think I was anywhere but right here at the table," Jane said. Cold rain had found a way under the hood of her poncho and was trickling down the side of her neck.

"Didn't I see you walk over to the far end to put your scraps in that wastebasket that was over there? It might have fallen off then."

Jane inched her way carefully, making small sweeps of the ground with her flashlight. "Here is it!" she called. "Thank goodness! I wonder if it still— Oh, my God!"

She'd held the watch up to her ear with her left hand while ignoring where the beam from the flashlight was pointing.

"What's wrong?" Shelley asked.

Jane stood frozen and speechless for a moment, then whispered, "Shelley, there's a body here!"

Elghl

❖❖ "A what!" Shelley said, rushing forward and ❖ tripping over a rock.

"A body. A dead one," Jane said with a horrified croak.

Shelley got her balance and joined Jane. "Where? Stop thrashing around with that flashlight."

"I'm shaking. Here. See?"

"Sam Claypool," Shelley said. "Come on, we have to get Benson to call the police."

"I'll stay here," Jane said, trying to sound brave. "It's not right to just leave him here in the rain."

Shelley grabbed her arm in a painful grip and hissed, "Jane, somebody killed him. Somebody who might still be standing a few feet from us in the dark."

"Killed him!"

"Jane, look at his head. Look at the big, heavy frying pan beside it. The man didn't smack himself upside the head with it. Come on."

They scuttled awkwardly, but as fast as they could, across the campsite and down the rain-slick path. The skies had opened and were pouring down frigid, drenching rain that felt like wet sleet. Jane fell half-way down and ended up on her backside in the mud. Shelley made it to the bottom, turned to look for Jane, lost her balance, and fell to her hands and knees.

Picking themselves up with considerable difficulty, they ran toward their cabin. "Jane, we'll take the van to the lodge. Throw some towels over the seats while I find the keys."

Like a jerky automaton, Jane did as she was told. Shelley jumped in the car, gunned the engine, shot backward a few feet, reversed, and headed for the lodge at a ferocious speed. At the front door she slammed on the brakes. The van skidded, convincing Jane that they were going to crash right inside the building. But Shelley stopped mere inches from the porch.

They flung themselves out of the car and through the front door. Above the pounding of her heart in her ears and the thunder outside, Jane thought she could hear voices in the kitchen and headed for the doorway leading to it from the reception area. Benson and his mother were there, putting away plates. They looked up with obvious alarm.

"Benson, Sam Claypool's been killed," Jane said breathlessly.

"At the campsite," Shelley added.

Benson didn't waste time asking questions. He reached for the kitchen phone extension and dialed the sheriff. Edna said, "You both look like you're about to pass out. Come sit by the fire."

Jane glanced down. "We look like pigs. We're covered in mud."

"Then sit on the hearth."

They did so and sat for a long time just trying to get their breath back. Finally, when they were able to talk without gasping and without their teeth chattering, Edna said, "What's this about, then?"

Jane explained about losing her watch and going back to find it and discovering Sam Claypool as well.

"I don't mean to be indelicate," Edna said, "but how did you know he was dead? Did you take his pulse or try to determine whether he was breathing? Maybe he'd just fainted."

Jane cleared her throat. "His his eyes were wide open even though it was raining in his face."

"And his head had been hit with that big frying pan. Up high on his forehead. It was a bloody mess and looked sort of—" Shelley took a deep, shaky breath. "Sort of flattened out."

"Why did he stay there?" Jane asked Edna. "Or did he? Was he there when you left?"

Edna closed her eyes for a minute. "Yes, I think he was. I saw Benson speak to him when all the other guests had left."

"What were they talking about?" Shelley asked.

Edna shrugged. "I couldn't hear and probably wouldn't have paid attention anyway. Where *is* Benson?"

"Right here," he said from the kitchen door. He'd dressed in waterproof clothing and was heading for the front door.

"Don't you dare go up there by yourself," Edna said.

"Mom, I'm not crazy. I'm going up with the sheriff when he gets here."

"And I'm going to take a shower and go to bed," Shelley said firmly, even though her chin was still trembling with cold and fright.

"But the police will want to talk to you," Edna said.

"Then they'll have to talk to me when I'm in my jammies," Shelley said. "I've never been so cold and uncomfortable in my life. And we left a fire in the fireplace because we thought we'd be right back."

Edna tried to keep them with offers of hot coffee, dry clothes, and beds in the lodge, but Jane and Shelley were both determined to go "home," to their own cabin and clothes.

"At least wait and let the sheriff see you safely into your cabin, and lock up really well," Edna warned.

Jane liked Edna, but was so miserable she was tempted to say, as Benson had, *Do you think we're crazy?* But she bit her tongue and followed Shelley out to the van, explaining to Benson that they'd like a little protection.

"I'll have Taylor drop me off with you and see you in safely, then walk the rest of the way."

It would have been polite to object to this self-sacrificing offer, but they were beyond courtesy. They waited in the van with the engine running and the heater going full blast. When the sheriff appeared, Benson hopped in the car with Taylor, and Shelley drove the van behind them. The sheriff not only took the time to see them inside, he quickly checked the bathroom, closet, and storeroom, made sure the glass doors were locked and drapes drawn, and they locked the door after him.

Jane and Shelley discarded their filthy, freezing outer clothing in the storage area. Jane said, "You're a faster shower taker than I am. You go first."

She put on her robe over her underwear and huddled on the floor in front of the fireplace.

Shelley walked into the bathroom door, and came back out a minute later in her long T-shirt nightgown. "I'm too tired. And I'm sick of water falling on me."

"Poor Marge," Jane said, her voice muffled by her pillow. She struggled up to a sitting position. "I wonder when they'll tell her."

"Not until they've taken the body away, I'd guess. I hope she doesn't have to identify it in that condition. I wonder where she thinks he is."

"Still at the campsite? Alive at the campsite, I mean," Jane suggested. "Or maybe she assumed he went on down to the lodge. It's not that late, you know." She held up the watch that had started their ill-fated quest. "It's only nine-thirty."

"No," Shelley said, then glanced at her own watch and said, "My gosh, you're right. It seems like it ought to be nearly dawn." She thought for a minute. "I haven't had time to really take this in, but who would want to kill Sam Claypool? He was such a boring, innocuous person. I can't imagine him rousing that kind of passion in anybody."

"Maybe it was that drunken nutcase, what's his name?"

"Oh, Lucky Smith. Maybe. He could have gotten

tanked up and figured it would really wreck things for Benson if a guest were found dead.''

''Kind of an extreme way to make a point.''

''That's why they call them extremists,'' Shelley said. ''Why don't you make us some coffee.''

''Because my legs have solidified. Give me a second and I'll do it. I wonder who else might be roaming around in the woods and up to no good.''

''On a night like this, not many,'' Shelley said.

''But you're always hearing about batty survivalists in remote areas.''

Shelley nodded. ''Yes, but I think most of them have their own land and warehouses for their weapons. I don't think they do much camping out in the rain in October. Although, for all I know, that could be their very favorite activity,'' she added with a wry smile.

''Should we go over to Marge's cabin when the police have told her?''

''A sympathy call? I don't think so. She's got her family with her. John and Eileen. I think it would be butting in. We can take her some food when we get back home. I guess we'll all leave tomorrow instead of staying on. Liz is going to be disappointed that she can't make a thorough report.''

Jane looked at Shelley. ''You're blathering.''

''I know. I need fresh coffee to slap around my brain cells.''

Jane hoisted herself off the floor and applied what little energy she had left to the coffeemaker. There was a small, high window at the side of the house facing the road. She could see occasional glints of light, but couldn't tell if it was distant lightning or flashlights in the woods. As she measured out the coffee, an official car of some kind went by silently but quickly.

Jane went into the bathroom, brushed her teeth and hair, and put on a flannel nightgown. As she went back to pour the coffee, there was a knock on the door that frightened her out of her wits.

"Don't open it!" Shelley said.

"Who's there?" Jane called.

"Sheriff Taylor, ma'am." It was the "ma'am" that convinced her. He came into the cabin, dripping like a sponge. "Did you ladies both see this body?"

"Yes. Briefly," Jane said.

"And you say it was Sam Claypool?"

Jane and Shelley glanced at each other, and Shelley replied, "What do you mean . . . we 'say' it was Sam Claypool? It was. There was no mistaking him. You met him yourself, earlier today."

"And exactly where did you see this?"

"At the far end of the campsite from the path we came in on. There's a semicircle of big rocks," Jane said. "Well, medium-sized. And he was just on the other side of them. Sheriff Taylor, these are odd questions. Why are you asking them?"

He sighed. "Well, ma'am, it's because there's no body up there. Not Sam Claypool's or anybody else's."

"*What!*" Jane and Shelley yelped in unison.

"Not a sign," he said.

"Somebody moved the body?" Shelley asked.

"Either that or . . ." The sheriff left the words hanging in the air.

"Or what?" Shelley asked.

"Or you imagined it," he replied bluntly.

"Neither of us are in the habit of imagining bodies," Shelley said angrily. "We're not lunatics!"

"I didn't mean you were," he said, not at all convincingly. "But it was dark, raining, you're in unfamiliar territory—"

"City slickers, you mean? Who can't tell the difference between a corpse and a pile of dead leaves?" Jane asked. She was as mad as Shelley. "We *saw* Sam Claypool's body. There was no mistaking it. We were standing only a couple feet from him. He was lying on his back. His eyes were open and he'd apparently been smacked in the head with a frying pan that was on the ground next to him. There was blood."

Taylor was shaking his head and glaring at them from under his heavy eyebrows. "We've had people here swear they've seen the ghost of a pioneer woman. It's easy out in the woods. There are strange shadows, animals, and tonight it was pouring down rain, there was lightning. It doesn't mean you're crazy, just that—"

"It was a body," Shelley said firmly. "If Sam Claypool's not dead, where is he?"

"I just sent my deputy to their cabin. We'll know in a minute or two."

Nine

"Well, he *is* missing," the deputy reported to the sheriff a few minutes later.

Jane and Shelley had dragged their bedspreads off the beds, and were huddled in them by the doorway where they were eavesdropping.

"See!" Shelley exclaimed.

Sheriff Taylor glared at her and turned back to the deputy. "When did he go missing?"

"His wife says"—the deputy consulted his notes—"that he said he wanted to just sit by the fire for a bit and told her to go on back to the cabin. She walked back with her brother-in-law and his wife and went to bed to read. Fell asleep and didn't even realize he still hadn't come back until I wakened her. Now she's in a panic."

"The couple in the cabin across from her are her in-laws. Better send them to her," Taylor said. "Keep her as calm as possible until we have this sorted out."

"That's it," Jane said to Shelley. "I'm giving up and getting dressed. We're not going to get any sleep."

Taylor overheard this. "Good idea. I'd like all you people in the lodge. My deputy will escort you down there when you're ready. Don't come outside unless he's here. Don't roam around anyplace on your own."

Jane closed the door, muttering, "Can we possibly look as stupid as he seems to think we are?"

Shelley looked at Jane, then down at herself. Both were clad in several layers of nightwear topped with matching bedspreads.

"Yes," she said.

They put on clean, dry clothes, but had to don the wet, muddy ponchos. The deputy—who turned out to be named Reedy, which was a serious disappointment to Jane, who wanted him to be called Fife— was waiting for them. The rain had again let up a little bit, but they hurried along as quickly as possible anyway for fear it would start up again. And it did, just as they reached the lodge. There were several unfamiliar cars parked in front, plus an ambulance, but no sign of the people who went with the vehicles.

Inside, most of the rest of the guests and staff, plus the ambulance driver and another police officer, were milling around. Allison wasn't in sight, but Benson, Edna, and one of the boys who had helped with dinner and entertainment had thrown together hot cocoa, coffee, and an assortment of doughnuts, apparently on the premise that a crisis always went better if there was plenty of food around. John Claypool was moving the sofas away from the fireplace and setting up rockers from the porch to hang clammy ponchos over to dry. He looked like a man who wanted to find something to do to keep his mind occupied.

Jane handed her poncho and Shelley's to him, and he arranged them neatly over the back of a chair. "You ladies found him, didn't you?"

"Yes, we did," Jane said.

"I should have gone back sooner," John said. "I told Eileen he'd stayed behind and I was concerned that he was worried about something."

"You went back to the campsite?"

John nodded and adjusted a few folds of fabric as if it were very important. "Went up there to see if he wanted to talk, but I didn't see him."

"And you didn't look around?" Jane asked.

John shrugged. "No reason to. He was sitting by the fire when we left. When I got back, he wasn't. I didn't have any reason to hunt for him. I just figured he'd gotten tired of sitting out there in the rain."

"Then what?"

"Huh? Oh, the rain was letting up, so I strolled on down here to the lodge and looked in the windows to see if he'd come here. Place was mostly dark, though, except for some light under the kitchen door, so I went on back to our cabin. I'm surprised I didn't run into you two ladies somewhere along the line. You sure he was dead? You couldn't be mistaken, could you?"

Jane shook her head. "I'm sorry, but I'm sure. Is Eileen with Marge?"

He nodded. "They aren't much alike, but they do get on pretty well. Poor ol' Marge. I don't know what she'll do without Sam. It's going to be tough on all of us."

Jane mumbled her regrets and, not knowing what else she could say to a grieving brother, went to join Shelley, who was picking over the doughnuts. "You might be interested to know that John Claypool was out roaming around in the rain this evening after we left the campsite," Jane said in a low voice. She repeated what John had said.

"So was Al Flowers. Maybe," Shelley whispered back.

"What do you mean by 'maybe'?"

"He was telling me he went out to their car to get something he'd forgotten to bring in. Said he'd bought an audiotape, some kind of music Liz hates and wouldn't let him play on the drive up. So he sat out in the car and listened to it by himself. Had the engine running and the heater on and said it was warmer and drier than the cabin."

"Did he see anyone suspicious?"

"He says he was listening with his eyes closed and fell asleep."

"It's probably true," Jane said. "But it is an odd thing to do on a cold, rainy night, isn't it?" She thought for a minute. "I wouldn't want to think badly of him. I like him a lot."

"Me, too. Jane, should we be telling the sheriff these things about John and Al?"

"I don't know. They'll probably tell him themselves. John didn't indicate that it was a secret anyway."

Shelley nodded. "No, neither did Al. Jane, why would anybody move a body? Especially a body that had already been seen by others."

"Maybe he didn't know we'd seen it," Jane said,

choosing a doughnut with chocolate icing. She
wasn't really hungry, just needed the comfort of
chocolate.

They took their coffee cups and plates into the
dining room, which was darkened. Nobody could
overhear them there.

"He?" Shelley asked.

"Well, I suppose it could have been a woman.
Sam Claypool wasn't a very big man, and I guess a
strong woman could have moved him."

"But what I can't get my mind around is why
anybody would move him," Shelley said. "Look at
it from the killer's point of view. Sam stays back
after the rest have gone. The killer creeps up on him,
smacks him with the frying pan—"

"No, wait. He probably wasn't still sitting by the
fire," Jane said. "If he had been, we'd have found
him there. Or John Claypool would have when he
went back."

"Right. Okay," Shelley said. "So the killer picks
up the frying pan— No, that won't work either. If I
were sitting out in the woods alone and somebody
came along and picked up a heavy frying pan, I
wouldn't stick around to see what they had in mind."

"Maybe the frying pan came later," Jane suggested. "We don't know what other injuries Sam
might have had. We didn't turn him over or anything.
How about this? The killer lures Sam away from the
campfire and into the complete darkness beyond it.
Maybe stabs him or knocks him out. Then, for good
measure, to make certain he's dead, gets the frying
pan and smacks him."

"Okay, but now comes the problem," Shelley

said. "If the killer wants to conceal the murder, why not take the body away right then?"

"He—or she—heard us coming? We weren't trying to be quiet."

"Possibly, but if he'd slipped back into the woods and watched us, why bother to hide the body afterward? We'd already seen it."

"But did we?" Jane asked. "Nobody seemed to believe us until they discovered that Sam was missing. Remember all that stuff the sheriff said about shadows and leaves and stuff?"

"That's the point, though. Even if they thought we were highly imaginative nutcases, Sam Claypool *is* missing. And if the murderer saw us discover the body, he wouldn't know that people weren't going to believe us. Unless the body disappeared, which it did."

Jane ate a bite of her doughnut, washing it down with some coffee. "And with all the rain, I'd guess any evidence of the murder and the removal of the body has been washed away."

"I hadn't thought of that. Yes, you're probably right."

"I did hear voices," Bob Rycraft said from the doorway. "I thought I was imagining it. What are you two doing in here?"

"Just talking," Shelley said. "Join us if you'd like."

"Thanks. I will. It's kind of a madhouse in the lobby. This is awful, isn't it? Do you think it was that weird guy who did it?"

"Lucky Smith? Maybe," Shelley said. "I hope so."

Rycraft looked at her oddly. "Why is that?"

"Because if it wasn't him, it was likely one of us," Shelley replied bluntly.

Bob Rycraft put his hand over his mouth for a second, a strangely childish gesture. "No! I see what you mean, but it couldn't be one of us! It had to be him—or one of his followers."

"You're probably right," Shelley said, sounding tired.

Jane saw some light from the dining room windows. She got up to look. Several figures were in the wooded area behind the lodge. They were apparently examining the ground with flashlights, moving slowly toward the path that led down to the lake. Looking for the body of Sam Claypool. A strange place to be looking, she thought. She and Shelley had seen the body at the other end of the property. Perhaps another group was searching that area, or maybe they'd already finished searching and were widening their area in desperation.

Poor Marge, she thought. To get word that her husband had not only died, but was missing besides. There was something doubly gruesome about someone hauling around a dead body.

She rejoined Shelley and Bob at the table.

"Bob said he went jogging after dinner," Shelley told her.

"In the rain?" Jane asked. "How miserable!"

"That's what your friend Mrs. Nowack said," he replied. "But if you're a serious jogger, you have to get your miles in whether it's convenient or not. I've gotten so dependent on it that I can't get to sleep at night unless I've done a couple miles first."

"Did you see anyone?" Jane asked.

"Nope. Not really. The Flowerses' car was running, though. No lights on, but the engine was running. I wondered why, but it was none of my business. Mr. Flowers told me he was listening to a tape."

"Have you told the sheriff's people that?"

"No, nobody's talked to me. They're all busy trying to find the—Mr. Claypool."

Jane felt a sudden and irrational flash of irritation. What was all this Mr. This and Mrs. That with him? Was he trying to make them feel old and frumpy or did he really think of everybody that way? Get a grip, she told herself harshly. He is young and very polite. That's all.

"I wonder how long they'll keep us all here," she asked.

"I overheard some talk between Mr. Titus and one of the sheriff's men about possibly setting up cots for us here in the lodge," Bob said. He said this cheerfully, as if he really thought an adult sleep-over would be great fun. Jane wanted to smack him silly.

Shelley put her head down on the table melodramatically and said, "Oh, no! I want to go to bed in a real bed! I'm *so* tired!"

Jane patted her friend's outstretched arm. "Well, if we have to sleep here, we're bagging spots next to the fireplace. Come on. Let's stake out our territory before someone else thinks of it."

"Good thought," Bob said.

They went back out into the lobby, which seemed like Grand Central Station after the quiet of the deserted dining room. John Claypool was pacing. Benson was messing about with the coffee urn. Allison had joined the group, and Edna was fussing at her to go back to bed, that there was nothing Allison could do to help and needed her rest. Liz Flowers was compulsively tidying the magazines set out around the room, putting all the *National Geographic*s in one pile and wildlife magazines in another. Al Flowers was reading an old newspaper Liz had apparently unearthed. Jane had grown so irritable that the rustling of it made her want to snatch it away, wad it up, and throw it in the fire.

"I'm losing it," she muttered to herself.

She and Shelley fought their way through the barricade of drying ponchos John had constructed and discovered the two ambulance attendants hogging the fire.

"*Do* you mind?" Shelley said in her haughtiest voice. They fled like frightened children.

They sunk into the sofas. A moment later, they heard the front door open and Eileen's loud, excited voice exclaiming, "They've found him!"

Jane and Shelley got to their feet and were peering over the curtain of ponchos as Eileen, grinning, flung the door wide open, and made a gesture like an emcee introducing a guest. Marge and one of the sheriff's men came in the door with Sam Claypool between them. He was soaking wet and covered with mud, but standing upright, and smiling tentatively, as if confused by all the hubbub.

He showed no signs of any injury whatsoever.

Ten

❖❖❖ Jane and Shelley walked back to their cabin in
  ❖ stunned silence. It was raining bucket-sized
drops and they didn't even notice. Nobody accompa-
nied them. Everyone had pretended to ignore them
when they left the lodge. Jane unlocked the cabin
door and they poured themselves inside, dripping riv-
ers. Still in silence, they undressed and got into
their beds.

Shelley flipped the light off, made a huffing noise,
and thrashed around in her covers. Finally Jane
said, "Shelley?"

"I can't talk about this, Jane. I can't even think
about it. We're both very tired. It's all a figment
of our imaginations because of sleep deprivation. Or
maybe we are asleep and this is all a dream."

"Yours or mine," Jane said wryly.

"Both, Jane. It could happen. It is happening."

"He *was* dead," Jane said.

"Of course he was dead," Shelley said angrily.
"Absolutely, positively dead. Then a few hours later
he was absolutely, positively alive. And in a rational

world, which I still steadfastly believe this is, that's impossible. Therefore, we are dreaming. I'm going to sleep now. More asleep than I already am. And in the morning, this won't have really happened.''

"But, Shelley—''

Shelley faked a loud, vulgar snore.

"Did you notice how nobody would look at us?''

Shelley snored again. Jane gave up.

Jane woke to the sound of the shower running and the smell of coffee. At first she didn't remember the evening before, then it all hit her. Shelley came out of the bathroom, scowling. She was still mad, but not hysterically mad. When Jane had showered and dressed, Shelley was almost calm.

"I've decided it was a trick,'' Shelley said.

"A trick? On us?''

"No, we were just the patsies who went along with it and helped it work.''

"So who was being tricked?'' Jane asked.

"I don't know. Somebody in the Claypool family, probably. Maybe Sam wanted to see what Marge would do or say if she thought he were dead. Or maybe it was aimed at his brother. Possibly they were in it together. I don't know. But I'm sure as hell going to find out. I don't like being made a fool of.''

"Then maybe you better keep this theory to yourself,'' Jane said, smiling in an attempt to keep the sting out of the remark.

"Why?''

"Because it's got more holes than a drawerful of my panty hose. For one thing, if it were a trick, it absolutely depended on someone seeing the body lying in the rain. That happened to be us, but only because I lost my watch. Nobody stole it, Shelley. It just has a clasp that comes undone every once in a while, and not even you knew that. Sam Claypool couldn't have known I'd come back to look for it. Nobody could have known that."

"You said John Claypool admitted going back."

"Yes, but he didn't see the body, he says. He was looking for his brother to be upright, alive, and sitting by the fire. He wasn't scouring every inch of the ground with a flashlight like we were. And nobody could have been expected to do that. Besides—"

"Besides what?" Shelley snapped, working up a temper again.

"He was dead, that's what."

Shelley made a whooshing sound like a balloon deflating. "I know."

"He really was, wasn't he? Is there any way in the world we could have been wrong about that? We didn't take his pulse or anything."

"Jane, you know the answer to that. He was dead. His lips were blue. His eyes were wide open. Nobody could fake that with rain falling in their face."

"Maybe he was unconscious. Can you have your eyes stay open then?"

"I don't think so. Anyway, his head was caved in at the temple. And there was blood everywhere. Although it's all washed away by now."

"There might still be traces of blood in the ground. Or underneath leaves," Jane said. "Forensic people can tell stuff like that."

"But why would they bother?" Shelley asked.

"Nobody but the two of us believes there *was* a body."

"Oh, of course," Jane said. "They all think we're nuts, don't they?"

"Wouldn't you? Come on, be honest, Jane. If I'd gone up there by myself and come back claiming somebody was dead and a little while later the 'body' walked into the lodge, grinning like an idiot, wouldn't you consider having me put away somewhere with nice soft walls?"

"But it wasn't just one of us. It was two intelligent, sober women with good eyes and no known history of insanity."

"Maybe that's it," Shelley said. "Maybe we weren't sober. We just thought we were."

"Uh-huh," Jane said. "Somebody siphoned a quart of whiskey into us while we weren't looking?"

"You don't need to be sarcastic."

"But I *do* need to. It's the only way I can cope with this. We aren't both crazy, Shelley, are we?"

Shelley considered this. "We *could* both go crazy, but it's unlikely it would be at the same exact time."

"That's reassuring."

"We didn't have any rye bread with dinner, did we?" Shelley asked.

"Rye bread? No. Why?"

"Because I've heard of whole medieval villages going crazy because their rye bread got moldy."

"Shelley, let's just pack up and leave. I can't bear to face those people again. After the big hoopla of Sam's appearance, they started darting glances at us as if they were considering turning into a lynch mob.

As if we'd made up the whole story of the body as
a tasteless joke."

"They'll get over it," Shelley said. "After all,
even if the man wasn't dead, he was sure a mess.
Something happened to him. He was a muddy wreck
and smiling like an idiot. No, we're not going
home yet."

"Aw, c'mon, Shelley! We've made asses of ourselves. And we've seen the place and done our job."

"Jane, most of these people are part of our community anyway. We can't get away from them by
going home. What if you have to talk to Liz in her
principal role about your daughter? You want her
thinking you're too batty to believe? Or if you need
a new car, which you assuredly do, and the best deal
is at Claypool Motors? Or if—"

"Yeah, yeah. I get it."

"And even if we didn't care what they think of
us, we have to sort it out anyway because otherwise
we'll go through life never knowing the truth and
wondering if we had simultaneous nervous break-
downs."

"Or rye-bread seizures. Okay, I know you're right,
but still—"

"We should have stuck around longer last night,"
Shelley said.

"Why? To give the sheriff the chance to arrest us
for malicious mischief?"

"No, to find out what Sam's version was of where
he'd been and what happened to him."

"Hmmm. That's right. He must have had to account for himself after half the county froze themselves looking for him."

Shelley took their cups to the bathroom sink, washed them out, and poured fresh coffee.

"Okay," Jane said, "let's remain calm and rational. First, when we go to the lodge for breakfast, I think we should be very agreeable. Almost, but not quite, apologetic about our 'mistake.' "

"We were *not* mistaken," Shelley said.

"You and I know that—or at least believe it— but nobody else does. We're not going to get any information if we insist on riding a high horse and saying we saw Sam's dead body."

"I guess so. They'd either be angry or feel sorry for us for being so stupid or misguided or whatever. But apologize . . . ? I don't think so."

"I know. Apologizing doesn't come easily to you."

"I just haven't had much experience. I'm so seldom wrong," Shelley said with a grin.

"Secondly," Jane went on, "we need to formulate a few logical, reasonable theories to account for a dead Sam Claypool turning into a live Sam Claypool."

"A miracle?" Shelley asked. She was cheering up.

"Logical, reasonable, etcetera," Jane said.

"Like what? If there were a logical explanation, we'd have thought of it already."

"Not necessarily. We've been too shocked at the apparent conflict of perceptions to study it dispassionately."

"You sound like a professor."

"I watch The Learning Channel, which is probably where you got that rye-bread theory. Now, seriously, there must be circumstances that could account for this."

"Give me an example," Shelley said.

Jane paced the room, thinking. "Okay—here's one. What if what we saw was identical twins?"

Shelley's laugh was more of a yelp. "Oh, Jane. If you're going to be ridiculous, apply your Learning Channel experience. Be more modern. How about if Marge has been saving Sam's toenail clippings and selling them to a syndicate of mad scientists who are cloning people?"

"I like it," Jane said with a smile. "Okay, what if the body was somebody else wearing a really, really realistic mask. One of those latex things."

"That's not quite silly enough," Shelley said. "But it is theoretically possible."

"Unfortunately, it brings us back to the same questions: why would anybody need to do that, and how could they have counted on us—or anyone else—coming back to be witnesses?"

"Okay—let me think this out. How about if somebody else was supposed to come back and be the witness?"

"What do you mean?"

"Well, suppose I was playing this trick for some reason. I might have gotten someone else to wear the mask, lie in the leaves, and all that. Then I'd come back here to the cabin, pretend I'd lost my watch, but was also sick at my stomach and asked you, as a good friend, to go look for it. I'd say I thought it might be on the ground at the far end of the campsite, and *voilà,* you'd find the body."

"And before that could happen, somebody else ac-

cidentally stumbled on it for another reason entirely?'' Jane considered it. ''Possible, I guess. So
we weren't supposed to find it, somebody else was.
But why?''

''Why is a different matter entirely. Right now
we're concentrating on how.''

''Okay, but if we imagine this realistic mask,
doesn't it mean Sam himself has to be involved in
the deception? Don't you need to model it on a
real face?''

''Oh, I don't think so. They have them made up
to look like famous people at Halloween. I'm sure
the President doesn't let some toy manufacturer come
into the Oval Office and make a mold of his face.''

''I guess this mask thing is a possibility, but we
can't get hung up on it and miss something else.
Shouldn't we go to the lodge and see if we can find
out where Sam says he was?''

''Right. But we have another stop to make first.
We need to go look at the place where we found
him,'' Shelley said.

''For clues?''

''For our own peace of mind.''

Jane opened the drapes before they left the cabin.
''Wow! Look at that! You can see the creek now,
it's risen so much. But at least the sun's trying to
struggle out and it's not raining.''

''Come on, Jane. I'm getting hungry and it's time
for breakfast. We need to look over the campsite
before all the good food is gone.''

There were no clues in evidence.
In daylight, they weren't sure precisely where

they'd seen the body. The whole site looked different. Rain had washed gullies and created weird little dams out of leaves here and there. The fire had not only gone out, but was a pool of nasty gray water.

But there was a spot just beyond the clearing that looked as if the wet leaves were a little bit more squashed down.

"He either got up and walked away or somebody picked him up," Jane said.

"How do you figure that?"

"Because there are no drag marks. Look." Jane put her foot on the leaves and pulled it back. It left a groove in the leaves and a muddy streak on the ground.

Shelley nodded. "But it rained all night, I think. Other leaves could have gotten washed out over such marks."

They examined the area thoroughly, even turning over leaves to see if there were any objects or signs of blood, but discovered nothing.

"What now, Sherlock?" Jane asked.

"Breakfast. We could move around a lot, sitting by different people, and see if anybody smells of latex."

Jane looked at her sharply. "You are kidding, right?"

Shelley drew herself up. "The rest of them might think we're crazy, Jane, but I expected you to know better."

Eleven

❖❖❖ Jane and Shelley felt awkward and embarrassed, and the others seemed to be feeling the
same. Benson welcomed them with a vague smile,
not quite able to look right straight at them. Edna,
who was tidying up the magazines in the lobby, un-
doing Liz's arrangements, suddenly had to rush away
on another errand after saying a quick "Good morning, ladies."

"I feel like we forgot to get dressed and nobody
wants to notice or mention that we're in our underwear," Jane whispered to Shelley.

"Remember that time the PTA board had the
meeting at your house and it wasn't until the meeting
was over that we noticed one of your cats had horked
up a hairball under the coffee table?" Shelley said.

"Oh, God! I'll never live it down. Yes, that's the
exact same feeling. We should have thought this out
a little better before we got here. How about pretending last night never happened?"

"Nope. You're the one who said we're taking the
line that we were mistaken and are vaguely sorry."

Breakfast today was a little more modest. Cereals, fruits, scrambled eggs, and toast were the primary choices. The room was also a good deal more crowded. Several more strangers had been added to the mix—young, athletic-looking people for the most part. Jane noticed that three of them at one table were talking quietly and looking at her and Shelley. Word must have gotten around about the batty pair who imagined dead bodies in the woods.

Everyone else ignored them. Nobody signaled them to join a table.

"Let's sit with Liz," Shelley said, fixing herself a bowl of cereal. "She'll either defend us or tear us into little scraps. Either way, we'll be done with the best or worst."

Liz and Al were sitting with Eileen Claypool and one of the new people. Jane and Shelley took their plates over and sat down.

"Good morning, everybody," Shelley said with shrill cheerfulness.

There was a mumble of greeting and the young man at the table was introduced as the boating instructor. Liz had been grilling him and went back to it. "What I'm getting at," she said to him, "is why lessons in driving around in a boat is educational? I'll grant that it may be fun, but the school district isn't in the business of providing fun."

Eileen saved the young man by responding, "But aren't school plays and concerts mainly for fun? And you offer driver's education, don't you?"

Liz wasn't impressed by the reasoning, though she wasn't quite as curt and accusatory toward Eileen as she'd been with the young man. "Plays and concerts, like most sports, emphasize team play, taking a specific role in society, and doing your best for the group. Although, to be honest, I believe far too much effort and budget are spent on both. As for driver's ed, almost everyone these days must learn to drive a car skillfully and lawfully.''

"But aren't all those things also fun for the students?" Eileen asked.

"Yes, but the emphasis should be on 'also.' Learning valuable life skills can be fun," Liz said. "What I'm questioning is whether lessons in boating aren't *just* for fun. Very few of our young people are going to become professionals in boating."

Eileen was digging her heels in, whether out of genuine philosophy or irritation with Liz, it was impossible to tell. "How many are going to become professional actors, or singers, or sports players?"

Liz backed off a little. "I'm sorry. I'm making you angry and I didn't mean to. But I am here as a representative of the school district and I have to look at the camp in that light. Are the activities primarily educational?"

"I understand that," Eileen said with a forced smile. "But what's wrong with having fun?"

"Nothing at all! So long as the tax monies that support the school district aren't paying for it," Liz said.

Then, in an obvious effort to change the subject, she said, "Quite an exciting night, wasn't it?" studying Jane and Shelley intently.

"Yes, it was," Shelley said blandly.

Jane started to get up. "Oh, dear. I forgot the cream for my coffee."

Without even looking, Shelley caught her sleeve and said, "You don't take cream in your coffee, Jane, dear. Sit down."

"Not even this once?" Jane asked. So much for escaping.

"No." Shelley looked straight at Liz. "Jane and I have realized that we were tragically mistaken in what we thought we saw last night. Although it would have been far more tragic if we had been correct in our perception. We are very . . . sorry to have upset everyone needlessly."

She said the words as if she were reading a press release.

Liz's eyes narrowed. "I see. And have you any idea how you made this mistake?"

"None whatsoever," Shelley said.

"Well, it certainly was upsetting," Eileen said. "Thinking Sam was dead. I guess that's why I'm feeling a bit cranky today."

"We really are sorry," Jane said. "We were only doing what we thought necessary considering what we sa—*thought* we saw. What did happen to him? Where was he all that time he was missing?"

"He's not sure," Eileen said, more mollified by Jane's apology than by Shelley's. "He said the last thing he remembered was sitting by the fire, and then he found himself by the boat dock, all muddy and cold and wet. He has partial amnesia, the doctor said."

"So they took him to the hospital?" Jane asked.

"No, he kept insisting he was all right and wouldn't leave here. So Benson Titus insisted that a doctor come to the camp and examine him."

"What did the doctor say?" Shelley asked.

"Just that he had a slight bump on the back of his head. Nothing serious. Didn't even break the skin," Eileen said. "But he said sometimes even a very slight head injury can cause temporary mental blanks, especially before and during the injury. Sam might have just hit his head on a branch while he was on the way back to their cabin, gotten disoriented, and wandered off."

"If he ran into a branch, wouldn't the injury be on the top or front of his head?" Liz asked.

"I guess so. It was just an example," Eileen said defensively. "Anyway, the doctor asked him a lot of questions like how old he was and where he lived and what he did for a living and what he had for dinner last night—that sort of thing—and he got most of the answers right. The doctor said the rest of his memory will come back sooner or later, mostly sooner. He wants him to have a skull X ray, but Sam says he'll do it when he gets home."

"You mean they're staying here?" Liz asked. "Why is that?"

"Oh, Sam's terribly responsible," Eileen said. It was hard to tell if she was praising him or complaining.

Jane realized that Liz was looking at her, not at Eileen. Jane forced her features to remain bland with a polite overlay of concern, but Liz's diamond-edged gaze disconcerted her. What was the woman thinking?

"I had an uncle who had that," the boating instructor put in. "He was in a car accident. Wasn't hurt a bit, but couldn't give the police his name.

They thought he was drunk at first. I think it took him a month or two to finally get it together. But he never could remember the car accident. It was strange. That's one of the reasons I'm studing psychology in college.''

This was the opening of the verbal floodgates. He went on at some length about himself, his studies, his current and past academic and social accomplishments, apparently secure in his belief that they found him as endlessly interesting as he found himself. For once, Jane considered this youthful self-absorption welcome, as it turned the focus of the conversation away from Shelley and her.

Liz, whose professional life was awash in young people, drifted away, claiming she was getting seconds, but reseated herself at another table. Al followed her example a moment later. The boating instructor droned on about himself. It was Eileen who reached the breaking point first. ''Excuse me,'' she said to him. ''Don't you have work to do today?''

''Oh, I guess I do,'' he said, unoffended. ''Nice to meet you ladies.''

''That boy needs to be smacked upside the head,'' Eileen said, watching him leave. ''Reminds me of the year our son nearly talked us to death. Motor-mouth, John called him. Then he stopped talking to us and it was all we could do to get him to speak. Kids!''

''Do you have other children?''

''No, just the one. He's twenty-three now, living in Maine, of all places. Does something we've never understood with computers for the government. I'm sure glad Liz Flowers wasn't the principal when he was in school. He took one of the district's first computer classes and had great 'fun.' It turned him around, gave him an interest in something healthy that led to better grades and a career."

Jane thought about mentioning that this was exactly what Liz was advocating, entertainment that was also useful, but decided it wouldn't go down well with Eileen in her current cranky mood—which she'd already blamed on them.

"What about Marge and Sam? Do they have children in the school district?"

Eileen shook her head. "No, they don't have kids. I think they both wanted them, but it never happened and Sam had a real prejudice about adopting, being adopted himself and all."

"He's not happy about it?" Shelley asked.

"He is, that's the weird thing. But he wasn't adopted as a little baby. He was in foster care until he was four or five or so. He won't talk about it, but it must have been miserable. You'd think being taken out of that situation and being treated like a little god by adoptive parents would make him feel just the opposite."

"They favored him?" Jane asked.

"Do they ever! He was a good student, never in any trouble, and when he started the car business, he did it on his own. Got a bank loan. Never asked for a cent from them. I didn't know him then, of course, and he's never said, but I've always thought it was because the very thought of owing them money would have been awful. Anyway, they thought it was great. Still can't stop talking about it. Oh, rats, I've gotten away from them and I'm still letting them get on my nerves. That's dumb.''

"How does Marge manage with them?" Shelley asked. "She doesn't seem to have—how can I say this nicely?—your 'backbone.' ''

"She manages fine. For that reason. Or maybe she's really stronger than I am. I don't know. She just does what they want her to, and goes on her way without getting her knickers in a twist. The minute somebody tells me what to do, I'm fighting it—even if I'd like to do it. Marge just goes with the flow. No nerves at all.''

Jane thought about this assessment for a moment. It was pretty much what Shelley had told her, too. But her own limited acquaintance with Marge didn't bear it out.

"She was certainly nervous last night. Early in the evening, I mean,'' Jane added hastily, not wanting to bring the subject back to the disappearing body. "She nearly had hysterics over seeing someone in the window the first night, and at the campfire dinner she was as jumpy as a cat.''

Eileen considered this. "Yeah, I guess you're right. But that was unusual. I guess it's just being in strange surroundings or something. I don't think she really likes this outdoorsy stuff. Wild animals and things. I'm not crazy about it either, but it doesn't scare me.''

Her voice had slowed and she was staring past Jane and Shelley. They turned to see what she was looking at.

Marge and Sam had come into the dining room, arm in arm. They were whispering to each other and smiling. Marge's fair face was flushed. Her tidy hair was slightly disarranged. She looked girlish and very happy.

"She doesn't look nervous today," Shelley said.

Eileen grinned. "No, she looks like a woman who just had a good bang."

After a few seconds of stunned silence, Eileen went on, "I can hardly believe it. I don't think I've ever seen them even touch each other, much less act . . . romantic. Amazing."

She started laughing. "Maybe all they've needed all these years was for Sam to get a bump on the head to make their marriage perfect. I might try that on John. Excuse me, please."

She got up and went to greet her brother-in-law and his happy wife.

Shelley and Jane stared at each other for a minute. "It could happen," Shelley said finally. "I suppose if I'd been told Paul was dead, and then found out he wasn't, I'd have been hanging on to him for dear life."

"So instead of being lying—and possibly crazy—scum, you and I have become heroines. The ditsy ladies who saved an ordinary marriage and turned it into something deliriously wonderful?"

Shelley cocked an eyebrow. "I think that's over-stating it a bit."

"I think it's nonsense," Jane said. "There's something going on here that has nothing to do with us. That man *was* dead last night, Shelley."

"Jane, as much as I hate to say it, we must have been wrong. Look at them. Just look! Sam is alive and well and looking like he might just seduce his wife right here in the midst of the cornflakes.''

''Sure. And what we saw was an amazing configuration of wet leaves that happened to look precisely like a dead Sam Claypool with his head bashed in,'' Jane said. ''Uh-huh. Sort of like those people who can see the face of the Virgin Mary on a pepperoni pizza.''

Twelve

❖❖ Benson entered the dining room and called for
❖ everyone's attention. He said he was going to
pass out a list of sample classes that the group could
attend or learn about. He introduced the instructors
individually, and the crowd that had slowly gathered
in the lobby and dining room, as local people who
had been invited to participate.

Jane and Shelley glanced down the list: Leatherwork, quilting, fishing, boating, local history, local
flora and fauna, bird-watching, aerobic exercise, swimming, language lessons—the list went on forever

"The school board and city council are welcome,
of course, to delete any of these they don't want and
add their own instructors and subjects," Benson said.
"This is just an example. Not all of these classes will
actually be held today. The asterisked ones indicate
literature only, which is being put out on a table in
the lobby. There are sign-up sheets out there, too. It
would help the instructors to know approximately
how many people to expect."

Jane glanced at the schedule. There was nothing

in the first two-hour slot that interested her. "I think I'll see if Allison is free to gossip about computer stuff," she told Shelley.

"You aren't dying to know about You and the Mammals?"

"Mammals, schmammals," Jane said breezily. "But I do want to go on the bird-watching hike if it doesn't start raining again. It looks like it will."

"Well, I'm going to the leatherwork class," Shelley said.

"Sounds kinky to me."

"It probably won't be, but one can always hope," Shelley said.

They went to sign up and unfortunately got behind Sam and Marge. Sam had his right arm around his wife and didn't let go even to sign up for the classes he wanted. They were so absorbed in each other that they didn't even notice that the women behind them were the ones who had announced his death. Jane noticed Sam was signing both of them up for several classes.

The first class wasn't to begin for fifteen minutes, so Jane and Shelley went back for another cup of coffee. Shelley looked thoughtful. "Jane, this must be costing Benson a considerable amount, bringing in all these people."

"Aren't most of them local?"

"Probably," Shelley said, "but he's still got to at least feed them and probably put a couple of them up for the night. He couldn't ask them to do this and then charge them for food and lodging. He's really going all out to impress us. It was very smart of him to invite the local people. It makes us seem less isolated. He's created a feeling for what this place is like when it's busy and full of people having a good time. Very clever."

"Shelley, what *do* you think of this summer camp thing?"

Shelley thought for a moment. "I'm not sure. I thought it was a great idea at first, but as irritating and belligerent as Liz is, she has a point. Parents or organizations *should* pay for summer camp unless it's primarily educational. Why should taxpayers fund it? If we were here on behalf of an inner-city school where the kids have little opportunity to really get a big dose of nature, I'd probably favor it. I guess it does come down to a question of exactly what *does* constitute education?"

Jane nodded. "I don't think anyone has a good fix on that anyway—despite Liz's views. We'll never go back to straight reading, writing, and arithmetic. And we probably shouldn't. I know my kids have benefited personally from some school activities that weren't strictly academic."

She spotted Benson nearby and interrupted herself. "Benson, Allison and I have a date to talk computers. I haven't seen her around. Next time you run into her, would you ask what would be a good time?"

"She told me. She's excited about talking to you. My mother and I aren't much into cyber-stuff, as she calls it. I'll check with her right now." He was back in a minute, to invite Jane upstairs to their private quarters.

"I'm off to do leatherwork," Shelley said. "Possibly to design an exotic garment that will shock and delight my husband. See you later."

The private quarters upstairs were wonderful, open and airy. There was a large central room that ran the length of the front of the building like the top of a *T*. Running back from the center was a kitchen and dining area. There was a big fireplace at the far end, which must have been directly above the fireplace in the lobby. To each side of the kitchen was a bedroom, sitting room, and bath suite. One was Benson and Allison's, the other Edna's. The perfect setup for both family life and personal privacy.

"This is fabulous!" Jane exclaimed as Allison showed her around. A counter ran along the entire front of the main section. There were six windows, with bookshelves between each, making them appear to be recessed, like dormers. At the far window, nearest Allison and Benson's suite, a very fancy sewing machine was set up. In the area behind it sat a huge quilting frame with a half-done red and green Christmas quilt on it.

The next window area was a desk for Allison's computer and printer. Cabinets beneath held paper, and the shelves next to it had a bookstore's worth of manuals. The third window contained a profusion of colorful house plants. A few of them were very fragrant, filling the large room with their perfume.

The other three windows, on Edna's end of the main room, were almost empty by comparison. A single old, well-shaped rubber plant was in front of one, a colorful miniature totem pole in another, and the third was bare. Edna's bookshelves were sparse, too. Only one was full, and it consisted entirely of paperback mysteries. Another had a pile of crossword-puzzle magazines, several dictionaries, and a thesaurus. Edna's end of the room contained an entertainment center with a big television, VCR, and cabinet full of videotapes, mainly, Jane noted, documentaries, musicals, and costume dramas.

"I could stay up here and never, ever go out!" Jane exclaimed. "You've got everything I love."

"We're lucky to be living now, aren't we?" Allison said. "I can be a complete hermit, but between the satellite dish and the computer, I'm also in touch with the whole world. What more could you ask?"

"Closer medical facilities," Edna said from the top of the stairs.

"Oh, Edna, no fretting, please. I'm fine," Allison said. "Jane and I are going to play on the computer."

"Have you seen that black knitted scarf of mine?" Edna asked.

"It's right here," Allison said, opening a drawer. "Some of the fringe was coming loose and I fixed it. What are you up to today?"

"Just prowling around," Edna said, wrapping the scarf around her neck. "Want to see how the classes are going. Benson's taken charge of the kitchen for the day." She donned a heavy coat, stuffed a pair of hand-knitted gloves in her pocket, and said, cheerily, "Have fun, girls," as she went back down the stairs.

"I've got a pot of coffee ready. Decaf, I'm afraid. Edna won't let Benson even buy the straight stuff for us."

"Why's that?"

"Because I'm not supposed to have any. I have a little heart problem, and Edna is determined to watch over my health whether I want her to or not. She's a dear, dear person, but I think she loves me too much. She never had a daughter, and my mother died before I even met Benson, so Edna's taken over being my mom. Unfortunately, she treats me like I were her beloved idiot child who requires constant care. She means so well that I can't bear to tell her I'm capable of running my own life.''

Jane didn't think Allison resembled an idiot child, but she did look like a sick woman. Possibly much sicker than she was letting on. Her coloring was anemic, she moved slowly and carefully, as if in slight but constant pain, and she spoke rather slowly, needing more breath to do so than most people. Edna was probably quite right to worry about Allison's health. She clearly wasn't well.

''But maybe she's right,'' Jane said hesitantly. ''About living closer to a good hospital.''

''Oh, she probably is,'' Allison said cheerfully. ''But I couldn't live anywhere but here. I'd wither away. And it would be even harder on Benson. This is where he's meant to be. He wasn't even upset about the land-restriction thing. I'll boot up the computer.''

They sat down side by side, and as the computer went into action, Jane said, ''What land-restriction thing?''

''Oh, I'm sorry. I assumed you knew. We were up front about it with the city council and school board. I didn't mean to be obscure. That crazy Lucky Smith—you know about him? He fell into religion about the same time he fell into the clutches of a band of environmental nutcases. He's never liked us since Benson had him arrested for being drunk in the

lobby the first year we were here, so Lucky figured
these people would help him with his revenge on us.

"I've researched this crowd since then. They'd
been part of Greenpeace, but were too militant even
for Greenpeace's agenda. They broke off and apparently go around the country, butting in to various
communities and causing trouble. It seems they're
top-heavy with radical but very bright, thorough law-
yers. For some reason, they descended on this county
and decided it should revert to wilderness."

"It looks pretty much like wilderness to me right
now," Jane said.

"No, there are buildings and people. I think we're
supposed to give the entire county back to the rac-
coons and possums," Allison said. "According to
them. So they moved in two summers ago, signed
themselves up as registered voters, and pushed
through a zoning regulation that was cleverly worded
to look quite harmless, but was aimed at ruining us."

"You and Benson specifically?"

"We are 'representative of the rape of the land,'
as one of their recent press releases said. According
to their regulations, we could continue to operate the
resort as long as we wanted. But we couldn't add
any additional structures—this was just as we were
completing the Conference Center—and we couldn't
'increase the drain on public resources.' I believe
that's how it was worded."

"What's that mean?"

"It means we can't increase our water or electrical
usage. And we can't even put in a water purification
system, because it would require an additional structure to house the machinery. Fortunately, by the time

this stupid thing went into effect, we'd already had one season's use of the Conference Center and the new bathrooms in the cabins, so the basic usage was based on those figures. But we can't expand—add new cabins or any new facilities.''

"Surely they can't dictate to you that way."

"No, they tricked the voters of the county into dictating to us. When it was all done and we realized what had happened, we consulted a couple of attorneys and it seemed hopeless. We could propose a reversal of the zoning and have it put to a vote again. But nobody but us was influenced by this—at the moment—and we'd have to conduct an expensive election campaign by ourselves, which we can't afford to do. The alternative is to defy the law, let ourselves be brought to court—they'd love to see that happen—and try to have the zoning restrictions declared unconstitutional. Again, a huge expense with nobody to share the burden.''

"Surely you have friends and supporters who would help," Jane said. "All those neighbors who are attending your classes today, for instance."

"Oh, everybody's sympathetic. They're not to blame for this situation. The wording of the vote was so deceptively innocuous, we all fell for it. Even Benson thought it only meant that nobody abutting our land would be able to put in a sleazy trailer park or a garish tourist trap. He voted for it. When we discovered what it really meant, and the environmentalists got their way and started announcing openly that they were targeting us as an example, all our friends and neighbors rallied around. But, Jane, these aren't wealthy people. Many are retirees on limited incomes. A great many of those who do have the money to help are really Chicagoans who have a second home here and can't vote. And frankly, most people in the county still don't grasp that it's going to happen to them as well when the group is through with us. They see it as a vendetta against us, which they sincerely regret, but refuse to understand that we're just the test case."

"You don't seem as angry as I'd be about this," Jane said.

Allison smiled. "I'm not supposed to allow myself to get angry. And while I am furious at anyone else taking away our freedoms, in purely practical terms, it isn't as bad as it sounds. We don't want to expand this place to be the equivalent of a Wisconsin Disneyland. We like it as it is. We didn't move here to get rich, but to have a good life. And that's what we've got."

Jane glanced around the big, warm, inviting room. "It sure is."

"   and even if we wanted to leave, we couldn't," Allison went on, punching some keys on the computer keyboard. "We can't sell it. Well, legally we can sell it, but then the utilities go back to ground zero."

"What does that mean?"

"That anybody who might buy it couldn't use *any* county water or electricity."

"My gosh! That's horrible. Could they put up windmills or something?"

Allison shook her head. "Nope. Those are structures. Forbidden. Our investment here has become, in legal terms, an enormous white elephant."

Thirteen

❖❖ "I'm so sorry to hear that," Jane said.

"Oh, don't be. I wasn't wanting pity. Just explaining the situation. Like I say, we very much resent strangers coming in and usurping our rights. But they're not really keeping us from doing anything that's important to us. Benson and I have no intention of leaving. We came here with the idea of living out our lives in this building. So the fact that the land is impossible to sell is really okay. We have no children to leave an inheritance to, so there's not that concern."

"What about Edna? What if she outlives both of you?" Jane asked bluntly.

"Oh, she's entirely likely to. She is, in her own words, a tough old bird. Edna also has quite a nest egg of her own. She inherited from a spinster aunt who was a whiz at investing. And Edna's no slouch at it herself. That's the only thing she's interested in on the computer. She buys and sells stocks through it. I guess that's really another reason we aren't as upset as we might be. If both Benson and I truly became infirm, we could give this place to a nature reserve and live on Edna's money. She'd like nothing better. She keeps begging us to let her buy something in Chicago and move back.''

''And you won't consider it?''

''Not now. Probably not ever, if we can help it. Edna's marvelous and wouldn't lord it over us that we were financially dependent on her, but we don't want that. And it all comes back, in the end, to the fact that we love it here. And we love our independence, even if we have to fight Edna for it,'' she added with a grin. ''So are you interested in seeing the stock program?''

The discussion was clearly over.

''Actually, I'd rather see what kind of games you've got,'' Jane said.

''A woman after my own heart,'' Allison said. ''Most of them are shareware. I'll make you copies and you can mail checks to the creators of the ones you like. I've got a great graph program, too. Do you knit or needlepoint?''

''Both. Badly.''

Allison laughed. ''Well, I can help you make absolutely beautiful charts. What you do with the actual work is your own problem.''

Two hours passed like minutes. Jane went away with a dozen disks with new games and a promise from Allison that if Jane would bring her laptop back later in the day, she'd see if she could figure out a few problems Jane was having with it.

''I have to take a nap after lunch,'' Allison said, ''but anytime after two would be fine.''

Jane went down to the dining room, where people were just beginning to drift in for lunch. Seeing no sign of Shelley, she decided to take her disks back to the cabin before she lost them. It was starting to drizzle and there was, once again, the faint, distant rumble of thunder. So much for bird-watching.

Shelley was in the cabin, changing her sneakers for boots.

"Make anything naughty out of leather?" Jane asked.

"Not unless you consider an eyeglass case naughty," Shelley said. "It was fun, though. The guy teaching it had all sorts of neat stuff to show us. I fell in love with a zippered notebook. I figure by the time I took lessons, bought all the materials and tools, and wasted half of them learning how to do this, I could have a really great notebook like it for just under two thousand dollars."

"Sounds like a bargain to me," Jane said, taking a towel to her hair, which had gotten damp on the walk back.

"Yeah, so I bought his for ninety," Shelley said. "Take a look."

"Wow, that is neat," Jane said. The notebook, a deep reddish brown leather, had a deeply incised paisleylike pattern all over it. "What are you going to keep in it?"

"You sure know how to ruin a good mood," Shelley said. "I have no idea. Important papers of some kind. Of course, if they're really important, it means I'd have to keep the notebook in the safe and not enjoy it."

"Then keep something really trivial in it."

"Nothing in my life is trivial, Jane. You know that. So what did you and Allison do?" Shelley asked, fondling her new notebook lovingly.

"Lots of computer things. She gave me a bunch of games to try out. And she's going to dink around with the laptop this afternoon to see if she can't kill that weird error message I keep getting. She's really good at this computer stuff. She's good at a lot of stuff, come to think of it. She's got a quilt set up in their big living room upstairs. Reds and greens. Really vivid, with what looks like thousands of little squares that form interlocking rectangles. She told me something interesting about this property, too."

Jane outlined the main points of the environmentalists' actions and the results.

Shelley was making little yelps of outrage as Jane spoke. "That's outrageous! It can't be legal! Why, I'd fight that tooth and nail."

Jane nodded. "You certainly would. And you'd probably win. But they aren't going to fight it. It's too expensive. They'd have to bring it to a countywide vote and promote their view pretty much by themselves. They don't have the money, and Allison's health wouldn't permit campaigning. Or they could flaunt the law and spend the rest of their lives and a fortune watching it grind through the courts. Besides, they don't mind that much."

"What? They can't improve their business and their investment's been rendered valueless and they don't *mind?* Nobody with the cash to have bought this in the first place can be *that* laid-back."

"They are. Allison says they have no children to consider. And Edna seems to be pretty well off on her own. And they don't consider their investment useless. They want to live here until they die.''

Shelley shook her head. "I don't believe it. I think they've just decided this is the official line they're taking with us.''

"Allison was perfectly sincere, Shelley. I'd bet my bottle of Giorgio on it.''

"Maybe so, but we haven't heard Benson's version. He's a very bright, ambitious guy in spite of his aging-hippie appearance. Look at the effort he's put into this sales job on us.''

"That's true.''

"And nobody gave him this place to start with. He must have paid plenty for it. Or maybe his mother paid,'' Shelley said.

"I don't think so. Allison made clear that Edna kept offering to move them to Chicago and support them, and Allison said they wouldn't consider it.''

"Where do you suppose he did get the money?'' Shelley said "He lived close to us once, didn't he say? And they were going to buy one of those houses that was supposed to go up behind our block. Those were to have been very expensive. Wonder what he did for a living.''

"You've got me there. I'll see if I can find a chance to ask Allison So I've been hiding from the group this morning. Are we still batty outcasts?''

"Nobody's said a single word to me about bodies, alive or dead,'' Shelley said.

"And have you thought of any new explanation?''

"I toyed with an international spy ring,'' Shelley said. "But it didn't work out. Couldn't figure out why anybody'd need to fake a dead car dealer. Then

I considered a big drug cartel transporting drugs inside the works of new cars, but that wouldn't account for the dead car dealer coming back to life. I can't come up with any explanation that makes the least bit of sense."

Jane put the damp towel back in the bathroom. When she came out, Shelley was standing by the glass doors overlooking the creek. "Look at this, Jane. Isn't that water getting closer to us? I don't like that."

"Hmm. Maybe. But it's still a long way below us. Don't worry. Your spiffy notebook isn't going to be washed away in a raging torrent."

"You know what I'm wondering?"

"I can guess. The same thing I am," Jane said. "Could all this stuff about the zoning restrictions have anything to do with our finding what was definitely a dead body?"

"Exactly. Or, even more likely, the environmentalists."

"How so?"

"They're trying to make the point of how much political power they can wield by ruining Benson's business. And he hasn't kept what he's doing a secret. He's invited half the county to come to these classes and demonstrations. Looks like it could be a very successful bid for the school to send their kids here and profit him considerably. That would wreck their plans, wouldn't it?"

"Okay . . ."

"So what could be more discouraging to potential 'investors,' which we are in a way, than to have one of us killed off?"

"So the victim was to be whoever was the last to leave, not Sam Claypool specifically?"

"Could be," Shelley muttered. "But—"

Jane ran her hands through her hair in a despairing gesture. "I know! I know! It still doesn't explain how he came back to life!"

When Jane and Shelley walked back to the lodge, the environmentalists were out in force. They were dressed in costumes. Animal heads that covered their heads, and black cloaks--for mourning, Jane assumed. They carried signs that said things like THE WILDLIFE WAS HERE FIRST! and ONLY FISH BELONG IN WATER.

"Do you think we could mention frogs also living in water?" Jane said under her breath. "Not to ignore newts and insects and all kinds of slimy things."

"I wouldn't mention anything to them," Shelley said. "I imagine every one of them can do a solid hour's worth of harangue."

One demonstrator had a large poster with a disgustingly vivid picture of a road-killed possum and the message SHAME! Jane turned away, revolted, and stuck close to Shelley, who was dodging through the line of protestors. In the distance they could hear a siren.

"Poor Benson," Jane said, entering the lodge. "They're trying to wreck this school project for him."

"But we're all smart enough to figure that out," Shelley said. "Still, posters like that picture could be really upsetting to impressionable kids. I hate myself for it, but I'm starting to have real doubts about the wisdom of sending them here."

Liz was standing by a front window of the lodge, watching the crowd outside. "Not good," she said when Jane met her gaze. "I don't like this kind of terrorism. Have you two had lunch?"

"Not yet," Jane said.

"Then come and sit with me, would you? I've been waiting for Al, but he's probably lost," Liz said. "The man has no sense of direction."

They got their plates and found an empty table in the far back corner of the dining room. "So how many of the morning-session classes did you get to?" Liz asked.

"Just one," Shelley said. "Leatherwork."

Liz cocked an eyebrow in disapproval. "Not exactly a 'preparation for life' class," she said.

"But I'm already prepared and have lived half of my life," Shelley said firmly. "And I wanted to know about leatherwork."

Liz knew another strong-minded, outspoken woman when she met up with one. She turned questioningly to Jane.

"Computers," Jane said promptly, glad she'd put away her game disks before running into Liz.

"That's odd. I dropped in on the computer class and didn't see you there," Liz said.

"Must have been while I'd stepped out to the bathroom," Jane said, smiling innocently.

Liz apparently accepted this and went on to enumerate the classes she'd dropped in on. She'd hit all the "worthwhile" ones. History, nature, wildlife of the area. But she'd also taken a glance at the outdoor, physical-exercise offerings—boating, swimming, gymnastics. Anything that had a hint of arts or crafts, she'd ignored.

Jane couldn't help but point that out. "Don't you like singing or dancing or making things?"

"I love them. Al and I and our kids all sing in the church choir, and he and I used to compete in ballroom dancing contests—until we started stiffening up," she added with a rare smile. She was stunning when she smiled. "I make a good many of my own clothes, and so does my daughter. But these are my pleasurable, leisure-time activities. I don't think they need to be taught in school. But I do try to keep in mind that this is only my opinion."

Jane smiled. *Not very successfully,* she thought.

"But this isn't really what I wanted to talk to you two about," Liz said. "I want to know about this body you found last night."

"We were mistaken," Shelley said. "Trick of the light, no doubt."

"That's right," Jane said.

Liz looked at them for a long moment. "Forgive me, ladies, but I don't believe that. What's the real story?"

Fourteen

❖ "Okay," Shelley said. "We did find a dead
❖ body. But since we were obviously wrong,
there's no point in talking about it, is there?"

"What made you so sure?" Liz asked. "That he
was dead, I mean?"

"You don't want to know," Jane said.

"I certainly do. That's why I asked."

Jane and Shelley exchanged glances, then took
turns enumerating the gory details.

"Hmm. Pretty convincing," Liz said, looking
sorry that she'd asked.

"We thought so," Shelley said wryly.

"Okay," Liz said, squinting. "There has to be a
logical explanation."

Jane felt a brief flare of anger. Did this woman
really think they hadn't even tried to determine what
the logical reason might be?

Shelley was thinking along the same lines. "Got
any ideas?" she asked frigidly.

"Not yet," Liz said, unaware of their hostility.
"Oh, there's Al!" She hopped up and went to fetch

him from the doorway where he stood blinking amiably.

"Okay, it's war," Shelley said. "We can figure out anything Liz Flowers can figure out, and we *will* do so first. How dare she question us as if we were a couple teenagers caught skipping gym class?"

"I'm going to do something I promised myself I wouldn't," Jane said. "I'm going to E-mail Mel about this and see what he has to say."

"Jane, he'll have a fit. You know he thinks we're buttinskies. And even if he is a detective, he won't be able to form any opinions without even having been here, much less seen the body. He'll think we're both crazy."

"Yes, but he is an expert on crime. He might have some ideas on how a person could look so thoroughly dead, then turn up alive."

Shelley shrugged. "He's your boyfriend, not mine. Go ahead if you think the relationship can take it."

Jane finished her lunch and went back to their cabin. The demonstrators had disappeared without any sign of bloodshed or scuffling. She hoped Sheriff Taylor hadn't planned a nice relaxed weekend at home. If so, it wasn't panning out for him.

After a laborious half hour, she'd written up a succinct description of what had happened for Mel and edited out anything that sounded hysterical. The whole story, she realized as she read it for the final time, was just plain bizarre. There was no way around it, no way to rationally explain the impossible. She plugged in the modem and, with a sigh, hit the Send button.

Then she shut down the laptop, closed its lid,

wound up all the various wires, and put it in its case
to take to Allison. The rain had picked up again, and
she had to resurrect the poncho raincoat, which was,
mercifully, quite dry now. She started down the road,
head down to keep the rain out of her face.

That's why she didn't see Lucky Smith until she'd
literally run into him. She should have been able to
smell him coming. He reeked of a mixture of booze,
sweat, and industrial-strength body odor. Jane pulled
back, tried to get around him. But he grabbed her
shoulder.

"I didn't do it!" he said.

Jane pulled away. She was more repulsed than
frightened, but there was an element of fear as well,
and bundled as she was in the poncho, carrying the
laptop, she had no free hand to fend him off if he
attacked her.

"You didn't do what?" she asked.

"Anything. I didn't do anything. Nothing bad.
They're saying I did it." He suddenly straightened
up, whirled around and headed back toward the lodge
at a drunken lurch.

Jane stood in the rain, breathing deeply, waiting
for her pulse to slow down. *I don't like this place,*
she thought. *I wouldn't come back and I wouldn't
let my kids come here.* It wasn't Benson's fault, but
after the last two days, she finally realized that she
couldn't support the plan. Educational philosophy
wasn't at stake, it was safety and peace of mind. This
was an area under siege.

There had been a mob at the lodge, wolfing down
a quick lunch before the first afternoon sessions. But

now it was nearly deserted, and Shelley was still sitting where Jane had left her. She signaled at Jane.

"I've been eavesdropping. Weird things are happening," Shelley said, when Jane was seated.

"You're telling me," Jane said, thinking of her encounter with Lucky Smith.

"Somebody set the boat adrift this morning. They had to call a neighbor across the lake to go out and fetch it back," Shelley said. "And all the straps on the life preservers are missing, as are the tapes for some exercise and dance thing they were planning. The front door of the Conference Center was locked and the key's gone missing."

"Somebody's playing silly games," Jane said.

"Yes, but why? Who?"

"The environmentalists?" Jane suggested. "They must have been hanging out in the woods this morning, getting ready for their demonstration."

"I don't know. Doesn't sound like their kind of thing. They're obnoxious, but like to get credit for it. Are you listening? What are you staring at?"

"Sam Claypool," Jane said.

He was across the room, with a cup of coffee and a legal pad, jotting down figures.

"Why?" Shelley asked.

"I don't know," Jane said. "It just seems there's something wrong."

Shelley gazed at him for a minute. "Doesn't look like it to me. He's just making notes. He looks perfectly content."

"Right, but . . . I can't figure out what it is. It's like my subconscious is trying to tell me something about him."

"Then tell it to speak up louder," Shelley said.

But Jane couldn't dredge up what it was that she found bothersome. As she watched, he picked up his legal pad and left. The dining room was nearly deserted now; only a few of the kitchen staff were left, eating their lunch before cleaning up. "I'm off," Shelley said.

"What class are you going to?" Jane asked.

"Just going to drop in on a few of them and stay wherever something takes my fancy," Shelley said.

Jane went upstairs and tapped very lightly on Allison's door. It was two o'clock, but Allison might have still been napping. The door opened a moment later. "Come in, come in. Let's look at your laptop."

It was soon apparent that while Allison understood the problem, Jane probably never would. "Why don't you go on and let me just fool around with this for a while and see what I can do," Allison said. "You'll be bored watching me, and I'll have the urge to explain things to you that you don't even want to know and wouldn't remember."

"Allison, if this is going to be a lot of trouble, I don't want to bother you with it."

"No, it's a challenge, and I don't have anything pressing to do this afternoon. I'll have it fixed in an hour."

"How'd you learn so much about computers?" Jane asked.

"I took a couple classes, just before we moved up here. Of course, they've changed enormously since then, but I knew just enough to keep up. I subscribe to several magazines and can always find help on the internet."

"What did Benson do before you bought the resort?"

Allison laughed. "Nearly everything. In fact, he worked for a while for Sam Claypool. He was a mechanic at his car dealership. While he was there, he got an idea for some kind of gadget for car engines. He worked on it in his spare time and patented it, then sold the patent to a car manufacturer. That's how we got the money to buy this place. Now, run along while I still remember what I want to try with your laptop."

Jane went downstairs slowly. Benson had worked for Sam. What a coincidence. Or was it, really? The car dealership was a huge one. Lots of people must have worked there over the years. She passed through the dining room slowly, deep in thought, and found herself looking again at where she'd seen Sam sitting a short time before. It was, she thought, the same place where he'd sat the night they arrived. He'd been writing on a legal pad that night, too.

Writing . . .

Jane gasped. Then closed her eyes and tried to bring up the image. Yes, that was what was wrong. Unless her mind was playing tricks on her. She had to be sure. Where was Shelley? She went to the lobby, riffled through some of the paperwork on the long table, and found the list of classes that were currently going on.

Campfire construction and safety. No. Shelley wouldn't be interested in that.

Hiking gear selection and care. No way.

Rappelling. Hah!

Beadwork. Maybe. Ditto a wildflower program.

Both were being held in the Conference Center. Jane pulled up her poncho hood and set out. It was pouring down rain again. Her mind was racing as she sloshed through puddles, head down to keep the rain out of her face. She passed a few people who'd apparently given up fighting the weather and were heading home. Though it was only a little after two, it was as dark as twilight. Except when the lightning flashed. She stumbled in the main door of the Conference Center and stood for a moment, dripping rivulets.

She heard a voice in a room opposite the dining room. She opened the door gingerly and the instructor smiled and waved her in. She glanced around at people who were strapping each other into rappelling gear. "Sorry, wrong room," she said, backing out.

She hadn't brought the class list along and had to roam the halls looking in doors. She finally located Shelley in the beading class, being held in one of the small rooms in the basement. "Come with me," she said to her friend. "I think I've figured out something, but it's so bizarre!"

Shelley didn't question her. She got up and excused herself to the instructor, put her poncho on, and followed Jane.

"Back to the lodge," Jane said. They raced through the rain, sending up splashes of muddy water. They stood on the covered porch for a second, letting the worst of the water run off.

Inside, they dumped their ponchos. "What on earth . . . ?" Shelley asked.

"We're doing an experiment. To see if you remember what I think I remember,'' Jane said. "I can't tell you without influencing your thoughts.''

"Jane, are you okay?''

"I'm not sure. Come in the dining room.''

It was deserted now. Lunch had been cleared up and they could hear voices and the sounds of dishes and silverware being put away in the kitchen. "Okay, Shelley, think back to the night we got here. Picture us sitting at that table by the fireplace.''

"All right.''

"It's after dinner, after Marge had hysterics about the face in the window, after dessert. Liz is trying to talk us into having a planning session. Where is everybody? What are they doing?''

"Jane, can't you just tell me what's on your mind?''

"No, I can't. It has to come from your mind.''

"Okay. Liz is pontificating. She's sitting here. Al's next to her, pushing dessert crumbs around his plate and saying, 'Now, Lizzie.' Bob Rycraft is standing with his back to the fireplace, hands behind him.''

"Good,'' Jane said. "Go on.''

"Benson wasn't in the room. John Claypool was sitting sideways, staring at the windows in the back wall. Eileen was filing her nails, which I thought an especially odd thing to do at the table. Marge was sort of huddled at the end of the bench, looking miserable. Sam was glancing up at Liz as she spoke and making notes on a legal pad. I thought he was pretending he was taking down what she said, but it was probably something entirely unrelated. He was ignoring Marge entirely, which was really insensitive, considering how upset she was.''

Shelley smiled. "I gave him an extended glare, which usually intimidates people, but I don't think he noticed."

Jane said. "Go sit where he was and pretend you're Sam."

"Jane, this is starting to get silly. Okay, okay."

She sat down, using a class listing sheet someone had left behind, pretending it was a legal pad. She gazed at where Liz would have been, jotting down imaginary notes with an imaginary pencil. "Is this what you want?" she asked Jane.

"Right. Exactly. Now, you sit here and let me take your place."

Shelley got up and watched Jane imitate her imitating Sam.

"Have I got it right?" Jane asked.

"Lean forward a little and tilt the paper a bit. Okay. Yes, that's it."

Jane grinned. "Now, go sit where we were a little while ago and close your eyes."

"You've lost your mind," Shelley said, but did as she was told.

"Now, picture Sam again this afternoon. Have you got your eyes closed? He's sitting in the same place—"

"But not so stiffly," Shelley said. "And not as dressed up."

"Right. Get the picture clear in your mind."

"I have."

"Open your eyes. Pretend I'm still Sam. Is this right?"

Shelley stared at Jane for a long moment. "No. It's not. There's something wrong."

"Does this make it right?" Jane asked, shifting the paper and imaginary pencil and pretending to write with her left hand.

Shelley's mouth fell open. "Omigawd! You've got it! He was writing right-handed the first night and left-handed a while ago."

"Not exactly," Jane said. "Sam Claypool was writing right-handed the first night. Somebody else was writing left-handed this afternoon."

Fifteen

❖ "What do you mean?" Shelley asked.

"Remember when I suggested the dead guy and the live guy were identical twins and you laughed?" Jane asked. "Well, I laughed, too. But I think I was accidentally right."

Shelley had come back to the table where Jane was sitting and they were speaking in hushed tones. "No, that's too absurd," Shelley said.

"Finding a dead body that's come back to life is an absurd problem. Only an absurd answer will explain it."

"Jane, maybe he's just ambidextrous. Some people are. I had a teacher once who could grade papers with both hands at the same time."

"But there are other things different about them, Shelley. The big one is that he seems to like his wife and she likes him. That surely wasn't the case the first night. They treated each other like slightly antagonistic strangers. The 'current' Sam is less stiff, like you said. The features are the same, but that stance is different. This one sort of swings his arms when he walks. The old one moved more like an automaton.''

"But something happened to him that gave him that temporary amnesia. Maybe the same thing just jarred him out of his stiffness.''

Jane didn't respond. She just looked at Shelley smugly.

"Furthermore, there are just the two brothers. Sam and John,'' Shelley said.

"Eileen said Sam was adopted, remember? How the parents had given up having a child, adopted Sam, and then along came John,'' Jane reminded her. "Sam could well have been a twin and they only adopted one of them. Adoptions used to be a lot different in regard to siblings being kept together.''

"Golly!'' Shelley said. "She did say that. Maybe you're right. If so, what do we do about it? Tell the sheriff?''

"I don't think Sheriff Taylor would believe us for a minute,'' Jane said. "I'm not entirely certain I believe it yet. Let's don't do anything right away. Let me get my laptop back from Allison, then we can go back to the cabin and figure this out in a careful, rational manner.''

"I'll meet you at the cabin.''

Allison already had Jane's laptop neatly tucked back in its carrying case. "Easier even than I expected,'' she said as she handed it to Jane. "A corrupt file. I deleted it and replaced it from my system.''

Jane gushed her gratitude, but Allison wouldn't have it. "It was nothing, really.''

"Oh, on another subject entirely,'' Jane said, "you

told me Benson once worked for the Claypools. You
don't happen to know if there were any other siblings
besides John and Sam, do you?''

Allison shrugged. ''Not that I ever heard of, but
we weren't social friends. Why do you ask?''

''Just wondering if there wasn't a brother or sister
to help them out with their parents,'' Jane lied. ''It
seems a shame they can't take more family trips
together.''

Allison looked at her oddly, and Jane, not wishing
to further compound an already flimsy story, thanked
her again and hurried away. The dining room was
filling up again with people stopping by for a snack
between classes. Jane grabbed a couple suspiciously
healthy-looking doughnuts and two apples. The parking lot was emptying as some of the local people
headed home early to start dinner or pick up children
from school.

When Jane got back to the cabin, Shelley had coffee made and looked sneeringly at Jane's food offering. ''What on earth are these? Oat bran doughnuts?''

''They might not be as bad as they look. There
wasn't much choice.''

''I think some governmental agency ought to make
food producers fess up that things labeled bran are
really low-grade sawdust.''

''So what do you think of my theory?'' Jane
slipped off her wet boots and poncho and sat down
cross-legged on her bed.

''I think it's loony,'' Shelley said. ''But so far,
it's the only one we've been able to imagine that
would explain the same man being both dead and

alive. But if Sam One, for lack of a better designa-
tion, is still dead, where is he?''

''Anywhere,'' Jane said. ''You could hide a six-
bedroom mansion with an Olympic-size swimming
pool in these woods. Hiding a body would be a
snap.''

''So did Sam Two kill Sam One?'' Shelley asked.

''I think he must have,'' Jane said thoughtfully.
''Sam Two was wearing the same clothes when he
was found as Sam One was at the campfire dinner.
He must have taken them off the body.''

Shelley shuddered elaborately. ''Yuck. Do you
think Marge knows?''

''That he's a different person or that he killed her
real husband?''

''Either one. Or—!''

''She was in on it!'' Jane exclaimed. ''Is that possible? Marge? Mild, quiet, scaredy-cat Marge a
murderer?''

''Maybe Marge isn't what she seems,'' Shelley
said. ''And maybe Sam One wasn't either. Suppose
their marriage had been really awful, much worse
than it looked to outsiders. She discovers that Sam
One has a twin—or maybe Sam Two did the discovering. Anyway, it could be to her advantage and
his to bump off Sam One. Marge gets out of a terrible marriage. Sam Two gets to step into his twin's
extremely well heeled shoes. And they're bound to
each other by the crime. Neither can rat on the other
without revealing their own part in the plot.''

''And they go off happily into the sunset,'' Jane
said. ''Holding hands and making a couple of neigh-

bors look like fools for imagining they found a corpse."

"From what we saw of them today, it's a very satisfactory bond," Shelley said, pouring them each a cup of coffee. "They couldn't keep their hands off each other this morning."

She thought for a moment. "But, Jane, there could be another explanation for that. Suppose there aren't two Sams. Just the same one. He had some sort of physical and mental crisis and it brought them together. You know, pouring out of true hearts and all that like Eileen suggested. A renewal of the love they must have had when they married. A second honeymoon, so to speak."

"But how do you account for the dead body we saw—and we both *know* it was dead—and the fact that Sam suddenly became left-handed?"

Shelley nodded. "I'm not crazy about the idea of Marge conspiring to murder her husband, though. She really seems to be such a basically nice, if downtrodden, woman. That scenario—physical and emotional crisis and so forth— couldn't Marge have been taken in by it, too?" She eyed the doughnuts for a moment, broke off a dainty piece of one and tasted it, then made a face.

"Marge is the one person who would know they aren't the same person," Jane said. "It would be hard to have a heart-to-heart talk about your marriage if the other person hadn't been part of it."

"Which is the reason for the amnesia," Shelley said. "If this guy is Sam Two, he could be telling her that he's the same old Sam, can't remember specifics, but has the vague sense that he's treated her badly all these years, has seen the light, and they're going to get a fresh start. Maybe even emphasize that he doesn't want to remember. That he wants to court her all over again, be young lovers.''

"Would you buy that?" Jane asked. She broke off another bit of the doughnut and nibbled.

"Not on your life. But then, I'm not timid, shy, obedient Marge.''

"I'll say! Yipes! This doughnut tastes as ghastly as it looks.'' She got up and threw the rest of it in the wastebasket. "Still, I don't believe Marge could be unaware that this is a different man. He looks the same to the rest of us, but without being too graphic—''

"Go ahead, be graphic,'' Shelley urged.

"I don't even need to. Different things happen to identical twins. Broken bones, scars, moles in different places. I'd imagine they develop different tastes—''

"Is this the graphic part?''

"Shelley, I'm serious. We all have things we like or dislike intensely for irrational reasons. Nature versus nurture and all that. Like me hating lima beans because I ate too many of them once and threw up at a school play. I wasn't born hating them.''

Shelley was staring off into space. "I saw a television show about this.''

"About lima beans or throwing up?''

Shelley rolled her eyes. "No, about twins. Wait, let me think for a minute. I think it was on one of those science and documentary stations. Some scientists or social workers had located a bunch of identical twins who had been raised apart from each other, without even knowing they had a twin. When they really dug into their very separate lives, they discovered that all of them were remarkably similar. They had the same sort of jobs—"

"I remember that, too! There was lots of stuff they had in common. They liked the same kind of music and colors and had even given their kids the same names."

"I wonder if Sam Two sings," Shelley said.

"I wouldn't be surprised," Jane said. "But, Shelley, if we're right about this, how in the world would we prove it? How could we ever get anyone else, particularly a backwoods sheriff, to believe it?"

"Marge would have to confirm it."

"If she's in on it, a coconspirator, there's no way she'd confirm it," Jane said. "And if, like you prefer to believe, she wasn't in on it and she just wants or needs to believe that this is the same man, it comes to the same thing. She's in love with this person, whoever he is. She's not going to help us put him— and maybe herself—in jail for murder."

"What about fingerprints?" Shelley asked. "Do identical twins have the same fingerprints?"

"I have no idea, but even if they don't, there's the problem of getting them," Jane said irritably. "Sam One's are surely all over his house, and we could grab a drinking glass or something that Sam Two has touched. But we can't get in their house. We don't know how to take fingerprints, and the sheriff has no cause to believe us and probably would need the fingerprint equivalent of a search warrant."

"So what do we do?" Shelley asked.

"I don't know. But at least we have a theory now.

A line of thought to pursue. We shouldn't be sitting here by ourselves, speculating. We should be hanging out with Marge and seeing what we can find out.''

"Right. But we only have until tomorrow. We're supposed to have an extended meeting tonight—"

"Liz's orders?" Jane asked.

"Who else? And then we're all leaving tomorrow."

"Then we better hotfoot it to the lodge and find out where they are."

"Probably in their cabin. In bed," Shelley said. "And if you think I'm—"

"If they're not around, we'll chat with Eileen and John. They know Sam well, too. Wait one minute, will you, while I check my E-mail."

Jane booted up the laptop and found Mel's response to her earlier note to him about the dead body that reappeared alive. It was a one-word reply. "Twins."

"Rats!" Jane said. "He wasn't even here and he figured it out before I did!"

The rain had let up again and there were even patchy bursts of sunlight from time to time. But as they approached the lodge, it appeared that there was a problem. A line of departing cars was stopped in the drive. The sheriff's deputy was directing those with drivers to back up and park.

Edna Titus was standing on the porch, watching and looking worried.

"What's going on?" Jane asked as she and Shelley joined her.

"The bridge has gone out," Edna said. "The creek came up and washed it away, I think."

"Bridge?" Shelley asked. "Oh, the one we crossed just after turning off the main road. Isn't there another road out?"

"There's an old logging road," Edna said. "But it takes a pretty sturdy four-wheel-drive even in dry weather."

"You mean—" Jane had started to say, *we're stuck here,* but that didn't seem polite. "You mean you're stuck with all these people staying here?"

"No, most of them are locals. The sheriff's put in a call for people around the lake with boats to come fetch them and take them home. They'll have to come back for their cars later."

Shelley cleared her throat. "Uh . . . I don't think any of the people with boats are going to take us back to Chicago."

"Well, no, I guess not," Edna said, clearly preoccupied with her own concerns. "But there's a daily bus to Chicago."

Shelley pulled Jane aside. "I don't like this."

"I don't like buses, period," Jane said.

"That's not what I meant. Jane, it's just occurred to me that we're miles from anywhere, stranded with one or more people who are murderers."

"You're right," Jane said quietly. "There is a great deal not to like about this."

Sixteen

❖ "I'm willing to reconsider the bus idea," Jane
said, heading for the front desk in the lobby.
There was, in fact, one remaining brochure about the
bus schedule, and she learned that it belched out of
the nearest town at two o'clock every afternoon. Today's means of escape had long gone.

"Jane, I want to get out of here, too, but think
about it," Shelley said. "We'd have to haul most of
our stuff in and out of a boat, beg a stranger to take
us to the bus station, and find our way home from
downtown Chicago at the other end of the trip. Then
we'd still have to drive back up here in your lousy
station wagon to pick up my van when the bridge is
fixed, and drive back home separately. Not a good
option."

"Better than staying here, though," Jane said.

"Not if we stick together. From now on, we're
attached at the hip."

"Swell," Jane said.

"I want to take a look at this logging trail," Shelley said. "Maybe the van could make it through."

"Right," Jane said sarcastically. "Or maybe, since a van is really a big empty box on wheels, it would slide down an embankment into the lake."

"Still, I want to take a look at it."

Eileen Claypool came into the lodge, looking around. When she spotted Jane and Shelley, she came over to them. "You haven't seen John, have you?"

Jane shook her head. "Nope. Is he missing?"

"Not exactly, I just wanted to tell him about this bridge going out. I don't like being stranded here. Benson has his staff out trying to hunt down all the local people to get them across the lake before it starts getting dark."

Jane was glancing around the dining room. "It's odd. None of our group seems to be here except for the three of us. Wonder where they all are."

"Marge is in her cabin," Eileen said. "I just stopped by there."

"And Sam?" Jane asked, barely managing to repress the urge to call him Sam Two.

"She didn't know. I thought maybe Sam and John had both come down here."

"Let's have a cup of coffee and see if they turn up," Shelley suggested.

"How's Sam doing?" Jane asked when they were seated at one of the dining room tables. By craning her neck, she could see a bunch of people heading for the boat dock. Not one of them looked the least bit happy to be going home by water.

"Fine, I guess," Eileen replied. "Marge said he feels okay physically, not even a headache, and is recovering nicely from the amnesia."

"I can't imagine why he didn't go home or to a hospital," Shelley said. "I certainly would have."

"That's because you don't have their parents," Eileen said, stirring two spoons of sugar into her coffee. "This is the first time in years we've all managed to get away from them. Believe me, it's like being sprung from prison. John and Sam both have to face going back and trying to get that dreadful house fixed up enough to sell it and get them into a nursing home. This is the only break they get before that project, which is going to be hideous."

"The parents don't want to go, I take it," Shelley said.

"God, no! That awful house is literally falling down around them, and they have it on the market for half again as much as it's worth. They think they're going to come live with either Sam and Marge or us. They're wrong! The house is disgusting. The carpeting is thirty-five years old and worn clear down to the backing in spots. The roof leaks buckets every time there's a mist. The plumbing is unthinkable. They're . . . frugal, let us say . . . about flushing unnecessarily and wasting water."

Jane and Shelley shuddered.

"Sam's tried to get cleaning people in," Eileen went on, "just to make it sanitary before they start their very own cholera outbreak, but the parents are obsessed with people spying on them and won't let the cleaners in the house. The parents think Marge and I should be full-time maids, nurses, and watchdogs. Fat chance."

"Where is this house? Close to you?"

"Oh, no. It's in a little town north of us called

Spring Oak. So every time we're summoned to take care of some imaginary crisis, it's at least an hour round trip."

"How awful for all of you," Shelley said. "I guess I wouldn't have given up a precious second of my only vacation either."

"In spite of it all, Sam certainly seems to have benefited from this trip," Jane said.

Shelley cast her a warning look, which Jane ignored.

"Oh, he has," Eileen said. "It's made him a new man." She said this without the slightest hint of irony. "Who knows—if he'd gotten away more often these last few years, he might have been a much happier, nicer person."

"And Marge seems more content, too," Jane said.

"Content?" Eileen laughed. "Maybe not the word I'd have used. Hot to trot, I'd have said. When I stopped by there a minute ago, she was in her bathrobe. In the middle of the day! This is not the Marge I know. I think it's sort of cute. A middle-aged woman going all googly-eyed over her own husband."

"What do you suppose made the difference?" Jane asked.

Shelley nudged her under the table with her foot. It wasn't quite a kick.

Eileen shrugged. "No idea. Just wish it would happen to me."

There was a sudden commotion at the door. Liz was using her professional-educator voice, with which she managed, without actually shouting, to penetrate the farthest reaches of the lodge.

"Where is the sheriff! Where is Benson Titus? I want to make an official complaint."

A deputy approached her. He tried to take her arm, but she shook him off. But he kept talking quietly while he led her into the dining room. As they got closer, the deputy could be heard saying, "Just sit down and relax for a moment while I find them."

Liz flung herself down on the bench next to Eileen. "I'm *so* furious!"

"What on earth's happened?" Jane asked.

Liz drew a long, deep breath. "Bob Rycraft and I went out to look over some of the grounds while the rain had stopped. I wanted to check out that area back behind the Conference Center. He would *not* listen to me about following the path to the right, so we went left and got lost. Male chauvinist pig that he is, he insisted I stay where I was while he tried another path. He never came back, naturally."

"Bob Rycraft is missing, too?" Eileen asked.

"What do you mean, 'too'?" Liz asked, but without waiting for an answer, she steamed ahead. "So I stood there for a minute, thinking the sun would come out again and I could get my bearings, and all of a sudden one of those dreadful costumed idiots came crashing through, knocked me down, and ran on. Just pushed past me like I was a bush! I fell backward and thought I'd broken my wrist."

She held out her right hand, shoving her sleeve up. Her wrist was swollen.

"You should get it X-rayed," Eileen said.

"No, I can move it. It's fine. But that's not all. I tried to follow this person and give her a piece of my mind—"

"It was a woman?" Shelley asked.

"I didn't know it then, but yes, I think so. I went stumbling through the brush and found her sitting on a stump, crying. Crying! It was that tall, gangly one with the stringy red hair."

"What was she crying about?" Jane asked.

"She claimed somebody had knocked her down, put a blindfold and gag on her, and taken her stupid costume. Stupidest excuse for an apology I've ever heard."

"You're sure it wasn't true?" Shelley asked.

"Oh, of course it wasn't," Liz snapped. "She'd gotten rid of the costume, of course. Probably threw it in the undergrowth when she heard me following her."

"And was there a blindfold?" Shelley persisted.

This took a little wind out of Liz's sails. "There was a long scarf that I guess *could* have been wound around somebody's face, but who would believe a story like that? I told her, you just come back to the lodge and try telling the sheriff this ridiculous story, and then I'll decide if I want to press assault charges against her. Stupid woman!"

"So she might have been telling the truth," Shelley said.

Liz gave her a first-class glare. "I'll tell you this right now. I'm voting against this harebrained scheme of sending our schoolchildren up here. This place is horrible. Just horrible."

"I agree," Shelley said.

"So do I," Jane and Eileen said in unison.

Liz was taken aback at last. "You do? All of you?"

They nodded.

"Then let's get out of here now," Liz said.

"Well, there's a bit of a problem with that," Shelley said. She tried to make it sound like she regretted giving Liz bad news, although Jane suspected Shelley was reveling in being the bearer of bad tidings. "The bridge has gone out. Didn't you see all the cars in front?"

"Surely there's another way out?" Liz exclaimed.

"There's a logging road that's probably flooded," Jane said. "Or you could wait in what probably is a very long line for a neighbor with a boat to take you across where you'd have to get a ride to town, then take tomorrow's bus to Chicago."

Liz muttered something that sounded suspiciously like "Oh, shit!" but wasn't quite distinguishable. Then she stood and beckoned imperiously to Bob Rycraft, who had come into the lodge looking discouraged and disheveled. His jeans were soaking wet halfway up his thighs. There was a swipe of mud across his forehead.

He hurried over to them. "Thank God you're here, Ms. Flowers! I found the way out, after I fell in the creek, and you were gone. I came back here to try to find a search party to go looking for you." His lips were a bit bluish and his teeth were chattering.

Liz was suddenly maternal. "Go to your cabin and put on dry clothes. You're going to catch your death. But let me ask you one question first. Do you still favor bringing the kids up here?"

Bob looked down, shuffled his feet. His sneakers squished. "Well . . . no, not like I did before all this. If adults can't even find their way around . . ."

"That's all I needed to know. By the way, how did you fall in the creek? It's on the opposite side of the lodge from where we were."

Bob's fair face flushed. "I got lost. I have no idea how I got there. I was following a path and had to dodge under a fallen branch and the next thing I knew, I slid into the creek and a black thing was wrapped around me. It was one of those black cloaks the protestors were wearing. Scared me out of my wits!"

All three women were staring at him intently. "Did it still have the mask attached?" Liz asked.

"Yeah, it was that falcon-looking one. It was stuck on a bush and the cloak was dragging in the water."

"And this took place on the other side of the lodge? Near the road where the cabins are?"

"Right," Bob replied, obviously perplexed.

"Then I've made a real fool of myself," Liz said.

Bob and Shelley both looked downright cheered by this unusual admission. Eileen looked at Liz as if she couldn't believe her ears.

Liz explained briefly to Bob about her encounter in the woods with the person in the falcon mask, although she left out the part about telling off the stringy-haired woman. "But it was only a few minutes between the person who ran me down and the woman I found. There's no way she could have gotten to where you found the costume and back in the interval. I guess I was wrong. Her crazy story must have been true. Go change into dry clothes, Bob."

"I'm going to go look for John," Eileen said when Bob had squelched off to his cabin.

Liz got a cup of coffee and rejoined them. "Why

would someone actually blindfold and gag one of those demonstrators just to get one of those stupid costumes?''

Jane and Shelley were silent. It was what they were both wondering, too, but they were unwilling to chat with Liz about their speculation.

Seventeen

❖❖ Liz suddenly remembered that she had threatened to file a complaint with the sheriff, which she now wanted desperately to withdraw, and rushed off to find the deputy she'd been ordering around.

Jane and Shelley were left alone in the dining room, except for a single waiter who was starting to set up for dinner. He put a tablecloth on the large table closest to the fireplace. The rest of the staff presumably was roaming the woods, rounding up stragglers and putting them on boats.

Jane refilled her coffee and said, "There's too much weird stuff going on."

"I'll say there is!"

"Completely apart from the business of Sam One and Sam Two, there's this mysterious person running around in a falcon costume, and there were all those strange things gone missing this morning. The aerobics tapes, life-jacket straps, and all that. But are they different mysteries or part of the same one?"

Shelley thought for a bit. "The only way I can see for them to be part of a whole is if the point is to ruin Benson's chances of getting the contract with the school board for the summer camp. And if that's the case, it's succeeded, I'm afraid. When even Bob Rycraft has lost his enthusiasm, I don't think there's a chance of it being approved.''

Jane nodded. ''And I feel bad about that because Benson is a nice guy who's gone to a huge amount of trouble to impress us. Even apart from the sabotage, it's too remote. The bridge going out is the final straw. It's bad enough that we're stranded here. But imagine if that happened when the kids were here and there was an emergency.''

''I'm not sure,'' Shelley mused. ''That discouraging us was the real point, I mean. Of course, it's what the protestors want, but the missing stuff and locked doors and all that were really trivial. Not nearly enough to make us vote against sending the kids. But I simply can't imagine the same mind that came up with those silly stunts thinking it would be a good idea to just murder someone at random to make the same impression.''

''I agree. Especially since Sam Two and Marge are the ones most apt to be involved in the murder of Sam One. They have nothing against Benson.''

''We don't know that,'' Shelley said.

''I guess not. But if we're right about the twin business—and I can't see how anything else can explain the dead Sam coming back to life—how could it have anything to do with Benson? Eileen has made it pretty clear that none of the Claypools are really the least bit interested in whether the school sends kids to camp. It was meant as a vacation for all of them, nothing more.''

"But didn't you say that Allison told you Benson worked for the Claypools? Then he invented the whatsisthing? Maybe that has something to do with it."

Jane looked doubtful. "It might, I guess. Maybe the Claypool brothers thought since Benson invented the thing while he was working for them, that they ought to have had some rights to the patent. It must have been pretty profitable if selling the patent gave him enough money to buy this place. But if that were true, why would anybody kill Sam to get back at Benson? That doesn't compute. Benson obviously wants this contract, but it's not a life-or-death thing for him. It's not as if his whole family is going to be reduced to begging on the streets if we decide against it."

Shelley ran her hands through her hair in a gesture of frustration. "I'm so confused!"

"I'm confused and frightened," Jane said. "Liz was just angry about getting run down by the person in the falcon costume. I think it's far more ominous than she realized. A person who would assault someone to get a costume away from them is definitely up to no good. I think somebody was frantic to conceal his or her identity, and that's scary."

Shelley glanced toward the lobby. "I don't like the fact that a bunch of us are unaccounted for. Sam and John are missing. And I haven't seen Al for hours."

"Shelley, let's go visit Marge."

"To what purpose? To ask her if she killed her husband, then passed off his twin as the same person?"

"Not outright," Jane said. "But if the subject comes up . . . ?" she added with a grin.

"If Marge is involved, I'd just as soon she didn't think we knew. A person who could bump off her husband probably wouldn't mind doing in a couple of near strangers."

"True. Okay, so we don't get near the subject. But I've never spoken to her except in a big group. I'd like to get more of a feel for what she's like."

"That's what's most wrong here," Shelley said. "Marge is a mouse. A very nice mouse. She's a mild, hardworking woman with no—"

"Personality?" Jane suggested.

Shelley nodded. "I just cannot imagine her involved in anything violent or illegal."

"Then let's go talk to her. Who knows? She might inadvertently say something revealing."

Shelley looked doubtful. "Okay, but don't say anything that will make her wary of us. She probably is already. We're the ones who shot off our mouths about finding Sam's body."

"Shelley, much as I hate pointing out the obvious, nobody believes us."

"But the actual murderer knows we're right—to point out the even more obvious."

Marge was no longer in her bathrobe. She was fully dressed, down to her boots. She seemed slightly alarmed to see them, or perhaps that was just Jane's imagination. She gave them a nervous smile and said, "Oh, hello," but stood her ground at the doorway.

"May we come in?" Jane asked bluntly.

"Well, I was just getting ready to go out and see where Sam is," Marge said.

"Oh, he's probably helping get people on boats," Shelley said.

"Boats?" Marge asked.

"Haven't you heard?" Jane said. "The rain washed the bridge out and the local people can't get home except by boat. Apparently all the neighbors on the lakefront have pitched in to evacuate them."

"How will we get out tomorrow?" Marge asked, reluctantly stepping back and gesturing grudgingly for them to enter the cabin.

"I'm afraid we might not be able to leave tomorrow," Shelley said.

Marge shivered. "I don't like this place. I want to leave. Surely there's some way to get out of here?"

Shelley explained about the logging road. "But it's probably impassable, too. Marge, if you don't like this resort, does that mean you'll be recommending against sending the children here?" she asked, just to keep the conversation going.

"Oh, I hadn't thought about that. Yes, I guess so."

"Does Sam feel the same way?" Jane asked.

Shelley glared at her.

"I don't know. We haven't talked about it really."

No, you've got other things on your minds. Sex and death, for starters, Jane thought.

"It's a shame," Shelley said. "Benson Titus has gone to so much trouble to impress us, but I don't think anybody favors the plan. Even Bob Rycraft, who was so enthusiastic at first, seems to have changed his mind."

Marge stared at Shelley as if forcing her mind back to the subject at hand. "I guess so," she said.

Silence fell.

Marge glanced at the door as if wishing it would open and some supernatural force would suck her out. Could a woman this timid, who couldn't even figure out how to get away from unwanted guests, be a party to murder? Jane wondered. It didn't seem possible.

Shelley said, "I guess you'll be at the planning meeting next Thursday." When Marge looked at her blankly, Shelley went on. "The park committee. Planning the new gardens around the city hall . . . ?"

"Oh. Yes. I will. I wonder— Well, I think I'll just run down to the lodge and see if Sam's there. If you don't mind . . ."

Trying to chat with her was obviously a lost cause. Marge was putting on her coat, and Jane went to open the door. She found herself facing Sheriff Taylor, his hand raised to knock. "Is Mrs. Claypool here?" he asked, obviously surprised to see Jane. A young, uniformed officer Jane hadn't seen before was standing behind him.

"Yes, she is. Go on in."

"I wonder if you'd mind staying," he said quietly. "My only female deputy is out sick."

"All right," Jane said, opening the door wider. She was bursting with questions, but this obviously wasn't the time to ask anything.

The sheriff stepped inside the cabin looking very grim. The young officer came in as well, closing the door and taking a notebook and pencil out of his pocket.

"Mrs. Claypool? I'm afraid I have bad news for you," Sheriff Taylor said.

Marge stood as if frozen in place.

"We've just found your husband's body."

"Wh—" Marge began, then clamped her mouth shut.

Which husband, you were going to say, Jane thought. She and Shelley exchanged a quick glance.

"It must have been in the stream and the high water brought it down to the lake," the sheriff said. "You won't have to identify it. Your brother-in-law already has."

Marge was still standing, statuelike, in the middle of the room. Her only movement was to twist a button on her coat. She had gone so white she looked like she might faint any second. Shelley gently took her arm, led her to a chair, and forced her to sit down.

"I'm afraid I'll have to ask you some questions," the sheriff said.

Marge kept twisting the button.

"You see, the body was naked—"

Marge drew in a sharp breath.

"It had a severe wound to the head. The left temple. And . . . well, he's been dead for quite some time." He turned to Jane. "It's the one you ladies found. At least, the wounds match what you described." There was the faintest hint of apology in his voice.

The sheriff's assistant was still standing quite still and unobtrusive by the doorway, already taking notes.

Marge had pulled the button on her coat loose and sat staring at it in her hand as if it were important.

The sheriff pulled another chair over and sat down in front of her. "I'm afraid there are a great many questions I'm going to have to ask you."

Eighteen

❖❖ Marge's story came out in fits and starts, out
❖ of order and with long intervals of sobbing. A
few minutes into it, John and Eileen Claypool arrived, distraught. John said, "Marge, you don't have
to talk to these people. I forbid you to. You need a
lawyer. Don't say a word."

Marge, her temper flaring for once, said, "I don't
need a lawyer, John. I haven't done anything wrong.
I'm sick of Claypool men telling me what I can and
can't do. Oh, please, please go away!"

John practically had to be thrown out of the cabin.
Eileen left in tears.

Sam Claypool knew he had a twin brother, Marge
said, between sobs. The boys had been in foster
homes together until they were adopted by different
families at the age of four. Sam didn't know where
his brother was and didn't care. His early childhood
had been so nightmarish that he wanted no reminder
of it . . . ever. He'd never even confided in John
about having a twin and had only mentioned it to
her once, on their honeymoon.

She had tried once or twice to get him to talk about it, perhaps even try to find his twin, but Sam was adamantly, almost violently, opposed to discussing it and accused her of betraying his confidence by even bringing up the subject. He obviously regretted having shared the information with her and was determined that she, like he, should block it out of her mind.

"Did *you* make any effort to locate him, your husband's twin?" Sheriff Taylor asked.

"Good Lord, no! Sam might have found out and would have been furious!" Marge said. "Sam had a—a bad temper. And it was his business, not mine. He made that very clear."

"So this person, this twin—what is his name?—found Sam," Sheriff Taylor said.

"Yes. His name is Henry McCoy. Yes, he wanted to find Sam. He'd had a hard life and some psychological problems that he thought might be solved by getting in touch with Sam. Reestablishing a family relationship," she said, as if it were a direct quote.

Henry had told her (just yesterday), she said, that he had spent three years just locating Sam. And then he'd had second thoughts. What if Sam didn't want to see him? What if Sam didn't even remember that he had a brother? They'd only been four years old when they were separated. An outright rejection might be far worse than the insecurity of having been separated in the first place.

So instead of approaching Sam directly, Henry McCoy tried to learn all about him first. He had, in fact, stalked his twin—not for any bad reasons, Marge insisted. Just to get to know him in a second-hand way so that he wouldn't make some dreadful gaffe when they did meet.

Henry took an apartment in Chicago and got a sales job with a farm implement company that allowed him freedom of movement, and started "studying" Sam, learning all about him so he could decide when and how to approach him in person.

He learned about Sam's car dealership—something he knew about since he, too, had been interested in car sales and had worked for several dealerships, but hadn't been an owner. He researched local papers for any mention of the Claypools and learned that Sam had been in a civic choir for some years. Henry, too, had a good voice and was interested in music. He started thinking they might get along well, with these common interests.

"Then why didn't he arrange to meet your husband?" the sheriff asked.

"Because Sam was . . . well, daunting. Very formal, rather cold. Except with customers."

"So Henry approached you, instead?" Taylor asked.

"Oh, no! No, he didn't," Marge exclaimed. "The first time I saw him, really saw him, was here. Looking in the window of the dining room the first night. In all those years I'd wondered about Sam's birth brother, it had never occurred to me, for some reason, that they might be *identical* twins instead of fraternal. And to see Sam sitting at the table in the lodge and the *same* person looking in the window . . ."

Jane remembered the moment all too well. If this was true—and she wasn't convinced it was—then Marge hadn't seen a scary stranger in the window.

She'd seen her husband's *doppelgänger*. Even though she'd known he had a twin, that must have been a horrible shock.

"You're certain you hadn't seen him before?" Taylor pressed the point.

"No. Really. But I knew there was something odd going on. Or at least I thought so. But I thought maybe I was going crazy. For about the last six months, I kept having the feeling we were being watched," Marge said. "We'd go to a movie or a concert and I'd have the sense that somebody was looking at us. And every time a strange car would park on the street, I'd think it was someone observing our house. It made me terribly nervous and upset. But I had no proof. Just a feeling."

She thought for a moment. "Maybe I had seen Henry before. One time I saw Sam in the grocery store parking lot. I guess now it must have been Henry. I must ask him about it. When Sam came home that night, I asked him what he was doing there, and he said he wasn't anywhere near the store that day. I was sure it was him and for some reason he was lying to me."

"Did you talk to Sam about it, the feeling of being followed and observed?" Jane asked. She hadn't meant to say anything, but it popped out. Sheriff Taylor gave her a quick, critical glance, but waited for Marge's answer.

"I tried to. Once. It made Sam so angry that I didn't mention it again."

"Why did it make him angry?" Taylor asked.

"Because he had the same feeling," Marge said. "Oh, he didn't admit it. But I'm sure that's what it

was. He was hateful about it. Said I needed to take
more estrogen, that I was getting the middle-aged
crazies. That I ought to see a shrink, except it would
be a waste of money. Sam wasn't—'' Her voice
caught. ''Sam wasn't a very loving person. Not affec-
tionate. But he wasn't nasty like that. I was stunned
by it. That's how I knew that he'd been upset about
being watched before I ever mentioned it. The only
other thing it could have been—'' She stopped.

''What's the other thing?'' Taylor asked.

''It's so stupid. I thought maybe Sam was the one
spying on me. Or somebody he'd hired was doing it.
Men his age sometimes get tired of their wives. And
it crossed my mind that he might be trying to—to
'get' something on me he could use to divorce me.
Something like an affair that he could use against
me. Sam . . .'' She paused and drew a long breath
and sat up very straight as if to brace herself against
her own words. ''Sam didn't really like me very
much, you see. I'm not sure he liked anybody. But
I really bored him. I think he only married me because I was pretty when I was a girl. And he wanted
a family. Children. When we realized—a long time
ago—that I'd never have any babies, he just lost
interest.''

Jane could almost hear her heart breaking for
Marge. Such a terrible admission.

''He wouldn't let me get a job,'' Marge said. ''He
felt it would reflect badly on him. Make people think
the car dealership wasn't successful . . .'' Her voice
trailed off.

''When did Henry plan on approaching your husband directly?'' the sheriff asked.

"I don't know. You'll have to ask him. Where is he?"

"I don't know yet. I have my people out looking for him now."

"Henry will tell you everything. He meant no harm, he was just nervous about how Sam would act when they met. It was terribly important to him that they get off on the right footing."

"And did they ever meet?" Taylor asked.

"No," Marge said with a shuddering breath. "Not alive. Henry found out about us coming up here to look over the camp. There was a little article in the local paper about this committee, you see. He managed to arrive a day earlier, hide his car, and set up a tent out in the woods somewhere."

"Why?" Jane asked.

Marge shrugged. "I don't know. You'll have to ask him. I guess he was just in the habit of watching Sam, maybe wanting to see what he was like when he was away from work. I don't know. He was in the woods that night—"

"The night your husband was killed? The second night you were here?"

Marge nodded. "Couldn't you feel it? That we were being watched from the woods?" she inquired of Jane, who made noncommittal noises. "Sam stayed back after the rest of us left. He didn't tell me why. Well . . . I didn't ask, to tell the truth. I was so uneasy myself that all I wanted to do was get to the cabin. Henry didn't say so, but I think he might have come out of the woods then and introduced himself, except that someone else came back."

"Who?" Jane and the sheriff said at once. This time he made a rude shushing gesture at her.

"I don't know. Henry wouldn't tell me. He said I was better off not knowing until—" She started sobbing again.

"Until what?" Taylor asked when her crying subsided slightly.

"Until he could prove what he'd seen."

"And what did he see?"

"He won't tell me. But he'll tell you. I know he will. He was only trying to protect me. He just told me he saw someone return and—and kill Sam."

The cabin was eerily silent for a long moment.

"Why didn't either of you just tell me this at the time?" Taylor said.

"Because I was afraid you'd blame Henry," Marge said. "Henry wanted to tell you. He knows who killed Sam, but he said the person had on gloves. That there would be no fingerprints on that frying pan."

"Did he say if it was a man or woman?"

Marge shook her head. "He was careful not to. But he'll tell you now. Now that Sam's been found."

"How did the body disappear?" Jane asked.

"Oh, Henry hid it and took Sam's clothes. He said the person who killed Sam would be so shocked at finding 'Sam' was still alive that he or she would get panicked, give himself or herself away."

"When did you find this out?" Taylor asked.

"Almost right away. Henry hid the body and came to this cabin. When he came in, I thought he was Sam. He was wearing Sam's clothes, you see. And his voice was the same. He said he had something very important to tell me. He was standing in a shadow. He said that when he got through telling me his news, he'd do anything I told him to. I had no idea what he meant. Then he stepped farther into the room and I realized he wasn't Sam.''

Shelley couldn't stand to keep quiet any longer. ''Are you saying you agreed to pretend to be married to—in *love* with—a man you'd never seen before?''

Marge had forgotten Shelley was there and jumped at the sound of her voice. ''I—I wasn't pretending,'' she said, tears starting to stream down her face again. ''He was the Sam I'd always wanted to love. The Sam that the real Sam never had been except the first few months we were married. Henry was warm, considerate, he really talked to me. He didn't frighten me. I didn't want him to tell the police anything. I wanted—''

She stopped and they waited. Finally Shelley asked, ''You wanted what, Marge?''

''I—I wanted life to just go on. I wanted Sam to stay disappeared. I wanted everybody to think Henry was Sam. I thought of the amnesia idea. In time, I could have told him everything about Sam's life. He could have become Sam. He knew about car dealerships and was good at math like Sam was. He could have stepped right into the business. We could have lived such a wonderful life if nobody ever knew.''

''Is that what Henry wanted?'' Taylor asked.

She shook her head miserably. ''No, he wanted to see justice done to the person who had taken his brother away before they could even meet. That's what he's out there now trying to do. Please, check with your people. See if they've found him yet.''

Sheriff Taylor didn't move. "My people will tell me."

Marge stared at him. "Oh, I think I see. Somebody else is already questioning Henry. You mean to compare what we say. That's okay. Really it is. Henry will tell the exact truth, just like I'm telling the truth. It is the truth, Sheriff. I swear it."

Nineteen

 "Do you believe that's the truth?" Shelley asked.

The two of them were back in the dining hall of the lodge and starting to feel that it was a second home that neither of them liked very much. Eileen had come back to Marge's cabin, insisting that she belonged at her sister-in-law's side. Marge had agreed that Eileen would be a comfort to her, now that she had become calmer.

The sheriff had abruptly dismissed Jane and Shelley when Eileen entered the cabin. He asked them, quietly but in a tone that was clearly an order, to go to the lodge to wait for him and not to discuss what they'd heard with anyone else.

They had no intention of talking to anyone else and had taken a table as far as they could get from both the kitchen—from which marvelous smells were coming—and the lobby, which was nearly deserted now.

"I can't imagine if she's telling the truth," Jane replied to Shelley's question. "If she is, it's about the saddest story I've ever heard. Imagine all those years with a man who didn't care about you and made no pretense about it. At least my husband sort of loved me—until he met the bimbo. It was one big, horrible shock to find out about her, but Marge has lived with an empty heart for most of her marriage. That has to be worse.''

"She could have left him, you know," Shelley said.

"Many women would have. But many wouldn't, too," Jane said. "She doesn't seem to have much self-confidence. She'd let her nursing credentials lapse, I imagine. She might have suspected that he was the kind of man who'd hire a very good lawyer and leave her penniless. She sort of hinted at that when she said she suspected him of having her spied on. Maybe she figured her life would be more awful and more empty and a lot poorer financially on her own. And she did say he wasn't usually terrible to her."

"But is that the truth?" Shelley asked. "Is any of it true? What if he was an abuser?"

"And she and his brother conspired to kill him?" Jane speculated. "Marge is obviously in love with this guy. And he is Sam's identical twin, with a lot of similar personality traits. Maybe he's just as much of a jerk as Sam was and has played on her loneliness. He stood to gain considerably. Everything Sam had, including his half of the car dealership, is now hers. She's probably a fairly wealthy widow."

"There's nothing like money to motivate people," Shelley observed.

"Do you think this is what this is about? Money?"

"And sex," Shelley said.

"She could be telling the absolute truth—as she knows it, or believes it," Jane said. "Because of her attraction to Sam Tw— I mean Henry. And maybe inventing bits to make him more sympathetic in her own mind. He's been observing both of them, not just his brother, it seems. Maybe he was really watching her? Trying to figure out whether he had a chance of sweeping her off her feet if Sam were dead."

"She did say she saw him at the grocery store. He must have known Sam wasn't with her then," Shelley said, nodding. "You could be right, that knowing all about her was every bit as important as knowing about Sam."

The young man who'd set the table by the fire came back with a coffee urn.

"Yes," Jane said, "he only had to know enough about Sam to figure out how to kill him and take over his business. But he had to make Marge fall in love with him at lightning speed. And he succeeded wonderfully. I'll get us some coffee."

When she got back to the table in the corner, Shelley was half-turned, staring out the window. It was almost entirely dark now and they could see the occasional darting beam of a flashlight in the woods between the lodge and the lake.

"We're assuming that Marge has been fooled and this Henry person killed Sam," Shelley said. "I'm not sure we should assume that yet. Suppose what she said was the truth? Who else might have killed Sam?"

"It's most often family members," Jane said. "That means John or Eileen . . . or both of them."

"Why?"

"Because they're family."

"No, Jane, I mean what could their motives be? Money?"

"Would they profit from his death?" Jane wondered. "Surely Marge inherited Sam's portion of the car dealership. John might be able to juggle the figures and cheat her a bit, but she probably had a pretty good idea of what their income was before and would sense if she were being cheated." Jane thought for a moment, sipping at her coffee. "No, I'm not sure that's right. Sam was a control freak to some degree. She probably had no idea in the world how much money they had. He struck me as one of those men who balance their wives' checkbooks and make them account for every penny, without any accounting in return."

Shelley nodded. "That would be my guess, too."

"But in that case, he probably had a will that specified some trusted accountant or banker to watch out for her interests. He's much more likely to have gone the paternalistic route."

"I'm losing the thread again," Shelley said.

"We're trying to figure out if John Claypool stood to gain from Sam's death. And I don't see how he could. Not enough to be worth killing for. And while they didn't seem exactly chummy, I certainly didn't get a hint of antagonism between them, did you?"

"No. I wouldn't call them close, but they worked together every day and have for years, so I assume they managed to get along."

"Simmering resentment?" Jane suggested.

Shelley shook her head. "John Claypool doesn't

strike me as a man who could simmer for long without boiling over. He's too brash. Too 'surface.' "

"I can't think of any other motive he'd have, then. Nor can I think of a single one for Eileen. If anything, this is to their disadvantage."

"How do you figure that?" Shelley asked.

"The car dealership apparently took two men full-time to operate. Now John's going to have to work harder than ever to keep it going."

"Mmm," Shelley said. "That's a point. Okay, if we're assuming that Marge's version of Henry is accurate, and John and Eileen are out of the suspect picture, who does that leave us? The rest of the committee."

"And the Tituses," Jane added.

"Let's leave them for a minute and consider the rest of the committee. What could Liz have against Sam?"

"I have no idea. Their lives don't seem to be likely to intersect at any point—unless she bought a car from him. Maybe a real lemon."

"Jane, if normal people killed salesmen who sold them duds, there wouldn't be any salespeople left."

"It was just an idea—I didn't claim it was a *good* idea," Jane said with a smile. "Couldn't be a flap relating to Liz's job. Sam and Marge didn't have kids."

"Al Flowers then?"

"I don't think Al Flowers could swat a fly, much less smack a person dead with a frying pan," Jane said. "And if Al were the type to take offense, he couldn't stand to live with Liz, who can dish out more offense in five minutes than anyone has the right to. And look how well he manages it.''

'' 'Now, Lizzie.' '' They imitated his rumbly voice in unison and laughed.

''What about money? You mentioned bankers a while ago,'' Shelley said. ''Car dealerships and banks go together. What if Al's bank was pulling some kind of monetary hanky-panky that Sam found out about? It could ruin Al and probably take Liz's career down with him. Schools can be awfully snotty about the reputation of their administrators—and their families.''

Jane looked down into her coffee cup. ''I've only known Al for a matter of days, and not well at that, but if this really is a world where somebody so nice can be a villain, I don't want to know about it. And would never believe it.''

''I know what you mean,'' Shelley said. ''I feel like I should get my mouth washed out with soap for even considering it. And I'd feel pretty much the same way about Bob Rycraft. Not that I'm so crazy about him, but I do think he's a bone-deep nice guy. He's a good daddy to a mob of little girls. If that isn't nice, I don't know what is.''

''So that leaves us with the Tituses,'' Jane said. ''I think we can exempt Allison. She seems to be in really frail health. I don't think she would have found it physically possible to lurk in the woods and deal a killing blow with a heavy frying pan even if she did have a motive. And I can't imagine what the motive might be. When I asked her about the Clay-pools, she didn't seem to show any interest in them at all except to mention that Benson once worked for them as a mechanic.''

"No guilty starts, gritted teeth, or furtive looks?''

"None of the above,'' Jane said with a smile. "She could be a fantastic actress, I guess. I'd swear that she was utterly sincere about how content she is with her life, though. She positively glowed when she talked about how much she loves this place, her quilting, her computer friends, her family. There's no room in the woman's life for a murderous grudge.''

"So what about Benson?'' Shelley said. "I wouldn't have thought he had a spare second to waste killing someone. I wish the sheriff had believed us and questioned everyone about their movements and alibis the night we found Sam dead. He was very likely with his family or staff the whole time after we left. There was a lot of cleaning up and putting away to be done.''

"That's a good point, Shelley. Now Taylor believes us, but everybody, including the murderer, can quite logically claim to not remember details of that evening. So much has happened since.''

"Tell me again about the patent business with Benson,'' Shelley said.

Jane repeated what Allison had told her about Benson inventing a mechanical gadget in his free time.

"So it wasn't part of his job for the Claypools?'' Shelley asked.

"She said he got the idea from something at work and invented it in his spare time,'' Jane said. "I don't know what the gadget was. I'm not sure Allison knows. Why do you ask?''

"Only because patents on inventions sometimes

become a lot more valuable with time. Suppose Sam had decided that he had some right to the profits because Benson worked for him when he invented it."

"What I know about the law would barely fill a thimble, but I'd guess it's too late. Benson sold the patent some time ago, and wouldn't Sam have to go after the patent office, or the people who purchased it, rather than Benson?"

"Maybe. The problem with this theory is that Sam and Benson hardly acted like they even remembered each other. I can imagine Sam concealing his feelings, but Benson? Not a chance. He looked like he was going to explode or have a stroke when Lucky Smith turned up here."

"Lucky Smith!" Jane exclaimed. "I'd forgotten about him. Now, he's somebody I can imagine getting tanked up and committing a senseless murder. And remember my telling you about him bashing into me outside and blathering about how somebody was blaming him for something he didn't do?"

"But nobody would have been blaming him then for Sam's death. Nobody believed us then that he was dead."

"No, Shelley, somebody *could* have been accusing him. Even if nobody believed us, Sam *was* dead by then. The murderer knew Sam was dead. And so did Henry McCoy—who might be one and the same."

"If you believe Henry's story via Marge, the murderer might *not* have known he succeeded in killing Sam," Shelley said. "He—let's say Lucky Smith—might have had only a dim memory of smacking somebody with something. I don't say Lucky couldn't have done exactly that, but I'm more inclined to think it was somebody blaming him for the silly stunts. The missing keys and such. For which he probably was responsible."

"It does seem his speed," Jane admitted. "We're not getting anywhere. Somebody killed Sam Claypool, and we're no closer to figuring out who he was."

"He or she," Shelley corrected.

"What 'she'? Who did we leave out?"

Shelley nodded toward the doorway to the lobby. Edna Titus was standing there, hands on hips, looking around the room.

"You two haven't seen Sheriff Taylor, have you? I need to find him."

"Why?" Jane asked bluntly.

"To confess," Edna replied with equal candor.

Twenty

❖   "Confess!" Jane exclaimed.

    "You killed Sam Claypool?" Shelley asked.

Edna looked at them as if they'd lost their minds. "Kill Sam Claypool? Me? Of course not. Why would I do that? I didn't even know the man, and I'm not a killer."

"But what are you confessing to, then?" Jane asked.

"A number of very silly, embarrassing things," Edna said, sitting down at the table with them. "I've made a fool of myself."

"How is that?" Shelley asked.

"My daughter-in-law is much sicker than she'd have anyone know. I do, by the way, trust that you'll keep that to yourselves. She has a serious heart condition, and I'm determined to keep her alive as long as I can. She must live near a good medical facility."

"Isn't that really up to her and her husband?" Shelley said.

"Yes, it should be. But they're so—so good, so naive. So blind to the hard facts."

"They're also very happy here," Jane pointed out.

"Allison isn't going to be happy when she's dead, and neither is Benson," Edna said harshly. "And she will be dead if she has a serious heart attack here in the woods."

"So you tried to sabotage our visit," Jane said, sensing that the moral position Edna had taken was probably wrong and certainly unalterable.

"Yes. I thought if I made things unpleasant and difficult, I might persuade your committee to vote no."

Jane and Shelley looked at each other, but said nothing.

"It was stupid and petty, but I have to save Allison," Edna said.

"How could this save Allison?" Jane asked. "Suppose you'd succeeded. This school thing wouldn't make or break the resort."

"Oh, it could," Edna said. "You see, the convention business isn't going well."

"Why not?" Shelley asked. "It's a wonderful facility for conventions."

"And it's hard as hell to get to," Edna responded. "Convention attendees have gotten spoiled over the years. They want open spaces, attractive settings, all of that, but they want to just get off a plane and be there. Or at least not be much more than a cab ride away from an airport. Nobody wants to land in Chicago, rent a car, drive for hours, and run a risk of getting lost. People will do that for a family vacation, but not for a convention. There's only one crummy bus a day to the nearest town, and purchasing and operating shuttles would be prohibitively expensive."

"Aren't there enough vacationers to fill the place?" Jane asked.

"Not since Benson built the Convention Center building. Vacationers don't want a dormitory atmosphere. They want privacy tho cabins in the woods."

She had lowered her voice. People were starting to wander into the dining room. The staff had apparently seen off the last of the local people and were now bringing out the metal containers and candles that would keep the food hot.

"Frankly, I can't agree with your motives," Jane said. "But you're right to tell the sheriff."

"I know. It'll be humiliating, but he needs to sort the wheat from the chaff now that he's got a murder to solve."

"Who do you think killed Sam Claypool?" Jane asked impulsively.

"I have no idea," Edna said. "And to be honest, I don't care. I just wish it hadn't happened here."

"I'm surprised you'd say that," Shelley said "What's more discouraging than a murder?"

Edna sat up very straight and glared at her. "I think that's a very tasteless remark."

"I think murder is pretty tasteless," Shelley replied blandly.

Edna rose majestically and left the table without another word.

"That's a pissed-off lady," Jane said.

"Yes? Well, so is this," she said, pointing at her chest. "How dare she set herself up as the goddess of Benson and Allison's marriage! She hasn't any right to run their lives that way."

"It's out of love for them," Jane suggested half-heartedly.

"That's not the point. Lots of people have done extremely damaging things out of love. It's wrong of her to decide what's right for her son and his wife. They've obviously made a hard decision, and it's up to them to make it and live—or die—with it."

Jane glanced up and noticed Sheriff Taylor entering the room. He was looking for them, but Edna caught him first. Holding on to his arm to keep him from escaping, she led him to the stairway. He made a quick *stay there* gesture at Jane and Shelley.

John Claypool and Bob Rycraft came into the dining room behind Taylor. They were obviously making polite discussion, and it was apparently agony for both of them under the circumstances. John looked haggard and tired and kept scratching his ankle. Bob was trying to strike a tactful balance between sympathy and his usual optimism—and failing badly.

The two men headed for the table where Jane and Shelley were sitting as if it were an oasis.

"We're so sorry about your brother," Jane said. "It's a terribly shocking thing."

"And I owe you ladies an apology," John Claypool said. He seemed to have aged a good ten years in one day. "I—we—should have believed you. If we had, the local law enforcement people could have gotten a much better lead on solving this horrible crime."

"It's perfectly understandable why nobody believed us," Jane said. "After all, it looked to everyone like Sam was alive and well."

"Marge must be insane," he muttered.

"Did you know Sam had a twin brother?" Shelley asked.

"God, no! Biggest surprise of my life. I guess our parents must have known, but they never said a word. Not a word. And Sam never mentioned it either. I can't figure why not. Jesus! How on earth am I going to break this to them?"

"Marge said Sam never mentioned his brother because he'd had a miserable life before your parents adopted him and he didn't want any connection with it, no reason to remember it," Shelley said.

"She told you that?" John asked.

"No, she told the sheriff. Has Henry turned up yet?"

"Henry?" John asked.

"Sam's twin," Jane explained. "His name is Henry Something."

"Oh, I didn't know. No. No sign of him that I know of." John's face was red with anger. "He's long gone by now. The bastard. Came in and killed Sam, wrecked our lives, got poor old Marge thinking she was an oversexed teenager, and then skedaddled the hell away when his crime came to light. Shit!" He caught himself. "Sorry, ladies."

"You're entitled to be upset," Jane said soothingly.

"How am I going to tell the folks? That's what I'd like to know. It's going to destroy them."

"You'll find a way," Shelley said. "Just don't make hasty decisions."

"So you're convinced Henry killed Sam?" Jane asked.

John Claypool's mouth fell open for a second, then

he sputtered, "Isn't everybody? Of course he killed
Sam. Good God! Here's this bum of a guy, God
knows what kind of criminal background, goes looking for his twin and discovers he's a rich, respected
man. All he has to do is knock him off and step into
his shoes. And his big house, and his business. The
deal even comes with a ready-made wife. My God,
Marge is nuts. Do you think she could have been
stupid enough to fall for it? Did she really think this
guy was Sam?"

"You'll have to ask her," Shelley said. "I imagine
she's telling your wife all about it now."

Bob Rycraft had slipped away after Jane and Shelley had let him off the conversational hook. Now Liz
joined them. She had Al in tow.

"Mr. Claypool! I'm so terribly sorry to hear about
your brother!" Liz exclaimed. "This is too horrible
to imagine. What can we do? Do you need any rela-
tives notified? How can we help?"

John was bowled over by her forceful offers of
help, and muttered vague thanks.

"I understand there was a twin brother masquerading as Sam? Did you know about him before?"

The conversation was a repetition of the one Jane
and Shelley had just had with him. Liz kept shaking
her head, looking enormously distressed. "I see
they're putting dinner out. I'll take plates to Marge
and Eileen. I'm sure they aren't interested in eating,
but they might want to just nibble a bit. Al, come
along. We'll get some plates and foil from the
kitchen and take them some food. Poor Marge."

"Marge is nuts," John repeated.

Liz dashed off on her errand of mercy, and Al

hung back for a minute, rumbling his own condolences in a low tone and adding that if there was anything the bank, or he himself, could do to help out, John wasn't to hesitate to call him. Then, at Liz's shrill summons, he ambled off.

"So the car dealership does business with Al's bank?" Shelley asked.

John shrugged. "I don't know."

"You don't know?" Jane said, thinking he'd misunderstood the question.

John's face, which had grown pale during Liz's forceful expressions of sympathy, turned red again. He scratched at his neck nervously. "No. See, I'm not a partner. I'm just head of sales. Sam owned the dealership lock, stock, and barrel. Now I guess I work for Marge," he added bitterly.

"Oh," Shelley said. "I've always assumed you were partners."

"Most people do. And Sam let them. I'd rather it didn't get around, really. God, I'm going to miss him. He was a tough guy to get to know, I guess. Kinda cold. I was the one always flapping my mouth and making jokes. But he was a good brother."

A heavy silence fell over the table. What was there to say?

"Let me get you some dinner," Jane suggested.

He waved away the idea. "Naw, I'm not hungry."

"But you should eat," Jane said. "You're going to need all your energy to cope with everything."

She dashed off to fill a plate for him. Liz and Al were just staggering away from the buffet table under a heavy load of food for his wife and sister-in-law. Sheriff Taylor and Edna reentered the dining room from the Tituses' private quarters. Edna's face was blotchy and her manner stiff and angry. Taylor must have read her the riot act, Jane thought.

"I need to question you ladies about discovering the body," Taylor said.

"Okay, but I don't want to leave John Claypool eating alone. Just a minute," Jane said. She found Bob Rycraft chewing on a chicken wing and trying to look unobtrusive, and ordered him, in the nicest possible way, to take his plate over to the table where John was sitting. She left the two men staring at each other and signaled Shelley to join her. They and the sheriff found a quiet, deserted corner in the lobby.

Taylor sighed wearily as they sat down. "Okay, tell me the whole thing, from the time you arrived at the campsite."

They told their story, jumbling it a bit and no doubt frustrating him to near frenzy. He kept asking about times, about weather, about where people were sitting. Now that he realized the importance of their information, he wanted every detail. But so much had happened in the interval that Jane and Shelley were no longer sure of their impressions.

"We had no reason to keep track of time," Jane explained, "and I'd lost my watch anyway. As for the weather, it had been drizzly all evening, but we were under a canopy and warmly dressed, so it didn't really matter to us."

"Okay," Taylor said. "Tell me about leaving the site."

"Sam Claypool had been singing—he had a great voice—and there was a big crack of lightning and a sudden downpour," Shelley said. "The young men who were helping with the dinner put their instruments away and started helping the Tituses pack up. It was frantic. Jane and I offered to help, but they insisted we were guests and shooed us away."

"Were you the first to leave?"

"I think maybe we were," Jane said. "I don't remember anybody in front of us. I do remember hearing Eileen behind us, complaining about getting her slipper wet."

Taylor refused to be sidetracked with slippers. "And when did you come back to look for your watch?"

Jane thought for a minute. "Not long at all. Maybe ten minutes?"

"More like fifteen, I think," Shelley said.

"Didn't give somebody much time, did it?" Taylor said, more to himself than them. "On the other hand, it didn't require much of an alibi time.

"Now, describe exactly what you saw when you found the— What is it?" he said to the deputy who'd come striding over and was waiting impatiently.

The deputy leaned down, whispering to Taylor.

Taylor walked away with him for a minute.

"Jane, will you stop that scratching?" Shelley said irritably.

"Sorry, it's like yawning. I see someone yawn and it makes me yawn."

Taylor came back and sat down at the table drumming his fingers for a few seconds, then waved the deputy off, saying, "I'll be right there."

"Something's wrong, isn't it?" Jane said.

"Yes, you could say that," Taylor said mournfully. "They've found Henry McCoy. Dead."

Twenty-one

❖❖ Jane and Shelley watched the sheriff leave with
❖ the deputy.

"I want to go home right now. This minute," Jane
said quietly through gritted teeth.

"Try telling that to the law," Shelley said. "What
a mess this is! Who in the world would want to kill
this Henry person?"

"Somebody who meant to kill him in the first
place?" Jane said. "Shelley, maybe that's it! Maybe
Henry McCoy was the intended victim in the first
place and somebody mistook Sam for him. Could we
have been looking at this backwards?"

"But nobody knew about Henry."

"Nobody *admits* to knowing about Henry. There's
a whopping big difference," Jane said.

"That pretty well leaves us with John Claypool or
Marge. And John, who might have had a good financial motive, just destroyed it by admitting he's
only an employee of the car dealership," Shelley reminded her. "He didn't stand to gain anything from
Sam's death."

"He could have other motives," Jane said half-heartedly.

"Like what?" Shelley said. "I'll admit I've tried to think of some and can't. If John Claypool had a gripe with his brother, I think he'd broadcast it far and wide. But Marge is looking like a better suspect every minute. If she and Henry plotted to bump off Sam, and then she decided the partnership wasn't such a good idea—"

"She's got a good alibi," Jane said. "Having been under police guard most of the day."

"But not all day. Remember when Eileen said she was looking for John and stopped at Marge's cabin and found her in her robe in the middle of the day? She was alone then."

"Had Henry, still masquerading as Sam, gone missing by that time?" Jane asked.

"I have no idea, but I'll bet the sheriff is drawing up a time line."

Al and Liz had come back from their errand of mercy and were filling their own plates. Bob Rycraft was eating with John Claypool. They'd given up any pretense of conversation. Bob was looking like he might nod off right into his food, and John was staring into space and taking an occasional bite of food. Benson and Edna were talking with one of the kitchen kids, and Allison was "circulating," visiting with the guests. It didn't look like anybody else knew about the latest body, and without even discussing it, Jane and Shelley were in agreement that they weren't going to mention it.

"I wish Sheriff Taylor luck with a time line," Jane said. "I'm glad it's his problem, not ours, and

I'm going to eat dinner before some new catastrophe catches up with this place.''

They both tried to force themselves to concentrate on food instead of murder. Tonight's dinner was ''home style.'' Pork chops, meat loaf, fried potatoes, scalloped cauliflower, Boston lettuce with choice of bottled dressings, cucumber sticks, Jell-O salad. Good food, but plain.

As they sat down, the sheriff came back into the dining room with Marge and Eileen in tow. Marge was sobbing; Eileen was trying to comfort her sister-in-law and shooting looks of pure loathing at Sheriff Taylor at the same time. Taylor was ignoring her.

''I'm eating my dinner, no matter what!'' Jane said quietly to Shelley.

Taylor came to the middle of the room and rapped sharply on an empty table for attention. This was unnecessary as everyone but Jane and Shelley was already staring at him.

''You should all know,'' he announced, ''that the body of Henry McCoy, who was passing himself off as Sam Claypool, has been found in the woods. He was stabbed to death.''

Somebody gasped.

Marge let out a low, shuddering wail of grief.

Eileen said, ''This is barbaric!''

''Yes,'' Taylor said. ''It is. And we're going to get to the bottom of it. Nobody is leaving this room until I say so. My deputy is going to give you pencils and paper and you're all going to account for your day. I want times, places, who was with you, who else you saw, what you did.''

He glared around at the owners, employees, and

guests. "When was the last time anybody saw Henry McCoy alive?"

Nobody said anything, and Jane reluctantly raised her hand. "Shelley and I saw him here, after the lunch crowd had left."

Taylor looked around. "Anybody else see him later? What was that time, Mrs. Jeffry?"

"One-thirty maybe? We didn't know it was going to matter."

"All right. So I want a detailed account of everyone's movements from noon until now," Taylor said. The man was in control, but obviously furious. "Everybody at separate tables, please. No consulting with each other."

Liz opened her mouth, glanced at Al, and snapped it back shut.

They sat obediently at their separate tables, writing, thinking, crossing out items, inserting others. John was idly scratching his shin. Al was tapping a pencil against his teeth. Edna was doodling around the margins of the page. Liz asked for a second sheet of paper for her opus.

It took around twenty minutes for everyone to finish the assignment. Taylor collected the papers, then addressed the group again. "We have people trying to get a temporary bridge in place so that police vehicles can get in and out. But nobody is leaving until I give permission. If you need to let anyone know why you are delayed, you may call from the front desk. Make yourselves comfortable here, because this is where you're staying for a while. The more cooperative and helpful everyone is, the shorter that time will be. I have my people posted at all the exits from this building."

Taylor took his pile of papers and left the room.

For a long moment everyone was silent, then several people rose from their isolated positions. Liz rejoined Al, Shelley came back to Jane's table, and Eileen rushed to comfort Marge, who looked like she was on the verge of a complete breakdown. Marge was so pale, Jane feared she was going to pass out. Allison was looking bad, too. She, Edna, and Benson were talking quietly. Benson patted her shoulder, then came to the middle of the room.

"Although my family isn't responsible for what's happened here, I'd like to express our most sincere regrets to all of you," he said. "This has turned into the Weekend from Hell for all of us. I just want you to know that I feel certain of what your decision will be about sending your students here for summer camp and that we don't blame you a bit."

He glanced at his wife, who smiled wanly and nodded.

"That's all, I guess. I'm sorry," he added, and sat down.

Jane went back to eating her now cold dinner.

The sheriff started calling people out of the room, one at a time. First Marge, who stumbled out like a disoriented ghost, then Eileen. John Claypool was next.

"At this rate, we're really going to be here all night," Jane said. "I've never been so homesick. If I start whimpering out loud, slap me out of it, will you?"

"Gladly," Shelley said. "Shouldn't we say something polite to Marge?"

"Like what? 'Sorry your husband died—again—and by the way, did you kill him'?"

"That might be a little tactless. But if she didn't do it, we're sure going to feel bad later."

Jane let herself be dragged over to the table where Marge and Eileen were sitting. "Marge, we're awfully sorry," Shelley said ambiguously.

"I've been widowed twice in one day," Marge said in a shaky voice.

They were spared having to respond by Eileen saying, "When this is sorted out, I'm going to make sure that damned sheriff is taken apart. This is horrible, making Marge sit here this way. She should be in bed. She should be under a doctor's care. The man is a savage."

She sputtered along in this vein for some minutes. Jane tuned her out. Eileen was right, of course, but Taylor had a bunch of strangers on his patch who were murdering each other. Because he hadn't believed her and Shelley the first time (not that he could be blamed for that), he was naturally determined to get all the facts he could now without any possible conspirators having the opportunity to consult with each other. She could sympathize with him for being angry—probably with himself, certainly with all of the guests.

Bored, and not wanting to talk to anyone else, Jane and Shelley went into the lobby where Benson had mentioned that there was a small library. They selected a couple of illustrated nature books and pretended great interest in them for the next hour.

Everybody was nervous and irritable. There was a lot of aimless pacing, very little conversation, and when a door slammed somewhere in the building, everybody jumped as if it had been a gunshot.

Jane and Shelley were the last ones to be called for their interview—and the only ones to be called in together. Taylor was in a small office near the kitchen that they hadn't seen on their tour. It was apparently where Benson did his bookkeeping and kept office supplies and guest ledgers. The desk was covered with the yellow legal-pad sheets they'd filled out earlier.

"Ladies, I'm going to make a leap of faith with you," Taylor said. "I got a call from a"— he rummaged through his notes—"a Detective Mel Van-Dyne, who is apparently a friend of yours you told about finding the first body. He was checking on your welfare, being unable to reach you by phone, and assures me that neither of you could be involved in this. I'm going to have to take his word for that."

"Thank you—I think," Jane said.

"Sorry, but I'm past good manners," Taylor said. "Now I'd like for you ladies to look over these other accounts and see if there are errors that you know of. Somebody who said they were somewhere you don't believe they were."

Most of the accounts were brief and vague. Apparently during questioning, Taylor had pinned a few of them down on times a little better because there were notations in the margins.

Not surprisingly, Al Flowers's was the skimpiest. He was a man of few words. He'd eaten lunch early, taken a nap, gone for a walk and, true to Liz's constant predictions, gotten thoroughly lost, but finally found himself at the far side of the Conference Center. He'd seen his wife walking hard on her heels toward the lodge and deliberately dawdled so he wouldn't catch up with her. He didn't wear a watch and had no idea what time it was then. Maybe two or three. Maybe later. Didn't see or hear anyone else.

Liz, in contrast, had detailed every moment. She recounted her mysterious brush with the person in the falcon costume, her return to the lodge, and eventually finding Al sitting in a rocker on the porch. She dragged him along on a hit-and-run investigation of the last session of classes.

Bob Rycraft said he'd attended a volleyball class right after lunch, then retold his version of losing track of Liz on their walk, getting lost, falling in the creek, returning to his cabin briefly, and coming back to the lodge to find Liz, after which he went back to his cabin and soaked in the bathtub until dinnertime.

"This person in the falcon costume is important, isn't it?" Jane asked the sheriff.

"I think so. Keep reading."

Eileen had lunch and went to the class session on beadwork, thinking she might learn something valuable to her business. Shelley confirmed this. Then Eileen said she went back to the cabin, thoroughly chilled, took a long, hot bath, visited briefly with Marge (who was in her bathrobe), and went to the lodge looking for John. Didn't find him there, didn't want to roam around the woods, so went back to their cabin, where he was reading the paper. Moments later, a sheriff's deputy arrived to ask John to come identify his brother's body. Eileen and John had gone to comfort Marge, been rebuffed by the police, fretted for half an hour, and returned to Marge's cabin, demanding to see her. She'd spent the rest of the day with Marge.

John reported that he had a late lunch, felt sleepy and tried to take a nap, but the bathroom faucet had a persistent drip, so he went out to their luxuriously equipped van and fell asleep there. He woke when he heard someone walking by, whistling, and went inside the cabin, where Eileen found him reading the paper.

Benson had a detailed account and collaboration from the staff, except for a brief period between two and three when he said he went for a walk, just for the sake of peace and quiet.

Allison said she hadn't left their private quarters all afternoon.

The kitchen staff all backed each other up for the entire afternoon.

Edna had apparently been difficult and refused to go into detail on her activities except to say that she had already confessed to her foolish tricks and had nothing to do with anybody getting killed. She also pointed out that she didn't have to talk to the police without an attorney present.

"You don't find that suspicious?" Shelley asked.

Taylor shook his head. "She'd already embarrassed herself in front of me, and I think she was angry with everyone else about it. I could be wrong, of course, but I've known Edna for a couple years and this is typical of her haughty act she puts on from time to time when things aren't going her way."

Jane waited until Shelley had finished reading the

last sheet, then said to the sheriff, "I'd have to study this again to be sure, but it looks to me like nobody is very reliable about what went on between two and three."

Taylor nodded. "That's true. That's why I was hoping you could substantiate any one of these stories."

"Only Eileen," Shelley said. "She was in a class with me at two o'clock."

"But you left not long after it started—when Mrs. Jeffry came to get you, right?" Taylor asked.

"Yes, and she could have left right afterwards as far as I'd know."

Jane flipped back through the pages. "During that time, Liz and Bob are getting lost and having adventures with the falcon person—or people. John Claypool's sleeping in his van. Eileen left the class at some point and went to soak in a hot tub. Benson's taking a solitary walk. Allison is fixing my laptop, though it could have taken her only a few minutes. Al's lost in the woods. Edna's not saying where she was."

Taylor nodded. "Right. About the only people who weren't 'missing' in some fashion were you and Mrs. Nowack. And the kids working in the kitchen."

Twenty-two

❖❖❖ *"What about Marge?"* Shelley asked.

"She didn't write it out, but says she and Henry McCoy went back to their cabin and he went off on a mysterious errand, promising to return in a few minutes. He never came back, she never left. According to her, that is."

Jane handed back the papers. "I'm really sorry we're not more help."

"Not half as sorry as I am for not taking you seriously when you claimed you'd found a body the first time." He rose wearily from his chair and said, "If you're ready to go, I'll have my deputy see you home."

"Speaking of home—our real home, that is," Jane said, "any chance of us leaving tomorrow like we were supposed to?"

He nodded. "Possible. Got a National Guard group putting in an AVLB."

"A what?" Jane asked.

"An Assault Vehicle Launched Bridge. It's more or less a tank with a folded-up bridge on top. They drive it into the creek bed and unfold the bridge. Two murders are officially considered an emergency. It'll take months to clear up the paperwork on the bridge, and the deaths will generate official forms for years." He put his head in his hands, muttering.

The deputy led them out of the room and waited while they picked up their belongings, with the rest of the group watching. "They probably think we're being hauled off to jail," Shelley said under her breath.

"Good. Let them think whatever they want," Jane said. "I think I'd rather be in a nice, safe jail than here. I want Aunt Bea to bring me breakfast on a tray."

The deputy tried to hide his smile.

He checked out their cabin so well, they nearly went mad, looking in closets, under beds, even in drawers, as if he suspected a bomb. He went out on the deck and examined the surroundings with a monster flashlight that could have done duty in a moderate-sized lighthouse.

"Is he ever leaving?" Shelley hissed.

Finally, mercifully, the deputy departed. "I never thought I'd wish for a television," Shelley said. "I want something mindless. Trashy, even. Something set in a city with lots of funny people who never heard of Wisconsin."

"I brought a bunch of books along," Jane said, fetching a backpack from the storage room. "They'll probably smell fishy forever. Take your pick."

Jane got herself set up with the laptop on the floor of the bathroom doorway—electrical plug for the modem going one way, telephone cord going the other—while Shelley rummaged through the books. She rejected the mysteries and found a beat-up paperback historical novel. She started a new fire in the fireplace and got her coffeemaker going. In other circumstances, it would have seemed like the coziest of evenings.

And they were both determined to pretend that was the case. "What are you doing with the computer?" she asked Jane.

"Just checking my E-mail and some internet addresses Allison gave me."

A little later, Shelley brought her a cup of coffee and hunkered down to look at the small computer screen. "What's that?"

"Real estate ads."

"You're kidding. There are real estate ads on your computer?"

"Mmm. These are things for sale in England. Look at the gardens on this one."

Shelley squinted. "Let's look closer to home."

"Planning to move?" Jane asked.

"I couldn't move. I'd have to clean the closets. I'm leaving that to the kids when I'm gone."

Jane punched some buttons, waited for another screen to assemble itself. "Okay, here's Illinois. What do you want to look— Oh, here's a listing for Spring Oak. Isn't that where the Claypool brothers' parents are?"

Shelley made a cross with her index fingers. "Do not speak that name to me!"

"Well, I'm curious," Jane said.

"I'm not. I hope I never hear of them again," Shelley said, wandering off to prod at the fire, which was creating far too much smoke and no warmth at all. "Paul says I should have been a firefighter since I'm so much better at putting them out than starting them."

Jane wasn't listening.

"Uh . . . Shelley. Take a look at this."

Shelley looked wary and she sat down on the floor next to Jane, who tilted the screen of the laptop. "Wow!" she finally said. "This can't be right."

The ad was for *"The Claypool Estate: a historic 12-bedroom, 7-bath Tudor-style mansion. Built in the 1920s by the grandfather of the current owner, this gentle old aristocrat of a home was fully updated in the 1960s, but needs renovations. Sited on 30 lush acres of woods, with a year-round stream and extensive gardens. Detached 4-car garage, with living quarters above; 6-stall barn."*

Jane dragged the cursor down and pictures appeared. The photographer had obviously done his best, but even the soft focus couldn't hide the cracks in the walls, the broken limbs on the trees, the general neglect and dinginess. "Notice what they *don't* say about it," Shelley said. "No mention of a kitchen, for instance. Real estate agents can wax rhapsodic at the nastiest kitchens. This one couldn't think of a single good thing to say. What's the price on this puppy?"

Jane cursored down again. Gasped. "Four million dollars."

"No wonder they can't sell it. It would take that much to clean up the place."

"Shelley, I think you're missing the point here.

These people are probably rich. The house is a mess because they've been too stingy to fix it up.''

"Oh. You're right. The way Eileen described it, I was picturing a run-down two-bedroom bungalow with a green plastic carport.''

Jane thought for a moment, trying to resurrect Eileen's many gripes. "She didn't *say* it was small. We made that assumption.''

Shelley shrugged. "Well, Marge is now half owner of a big, run-down house.''

"No, she isn't," Jane said. "She had every right to inherit from her husband. But he's dead and his parents aren't. That we know of.''

Shelley opened her eyes very wide. "Sam's death doubled John's inheritance, didn't it?''

"Unless they're planning to leave the whole bundle to an animal shelter," Jane said wryly.

"They could be very, very rich," Shelley said after a moment's thought.

"And they're very, very old and frail," Jane added.

"Where's that deputy?" Shelley said. "We have to tell Sheriff Taylor about this.''

"Just call the lodge," Jane said.

"Jane, you're *on* the phone line.''

"Oh, right. Okay, I'll write down where I found this.''

She did so and logged off. Then she called the lodge and asked for Taylor. "We need to talk to you," she said.

"First thing in the morning, Mrs. Jeffry," he replied, sounding very tired.

"I—I think it should be now.''

There was a moment's silence before he said crisply, "I'll be right there."

When he arrived, Shelley explained the background of their discovery while Jane booted up the computer again. "Eileen complained a lot about John and Sam's parents before all this happened. She said they lived in an old, falling-apart house that was for sale. We assumed it was a little house. Not that she actually said so. Then John Claypool told us that he wasn't an owner of the car dealership, only an employee—"

Taylor nodded. "He told me that, too."

"So we figured he had no financial interest in his brother's death—"

"Here it is," Jane said. "I'm afraid you'll have to sit on the floor to see this."

Taylor wheezed as he sat down, and his knee popped when he tried to fold himself into a comfortable position. He read the real estate ad. "This belongs to John and Sam's parents?"

"It must. It's the right town and family name."

"And the only child left is John," Sheriff Taylor said, struggling to get back up. "I'll check this out tomorrow."

Jane hadn't expected him to yodel or turn cartwheels, but she was disappointed in his matter-of-fact tone.

"But this is probably his motive," Jane said. "And he certainly had the opportunity. There's nobody to corroborate his story about taking a nap in the van."

Taylor sat down on the edge of Shelley's bed, massaging his knee. "You could be right. But motive isn't enough to convict. Any number of other people might have a motive that we either don't know about or wouldn't make sense to us. And nearly everybody here had the opportunity. You've seen the time schedule.''

"But—he admitted he'd gone back to the campsite the night we found Sam's body," Shelley said.

Taylor put his hands out helplessly. "Doesn't mean anything. Not legally. Ladies, I appreciate this information. It may help. But I'm not making an arrest until I have some kind of proof.''

Jane shut down the computer. "Do you think we're right, though?''

He folded his arms, looked down at the floor, and nodded. "I've thought so from the minute we found the first body. Unofficially, I'm positive of it. But this is the first murder—the first and second—in the last twenty years in this county, and I'm not making a move until I'm sure I can get a conviction.'' He stood up and headed for the door. "Lock up carefully.''

"He's right, you know," Shelley said when he'd gone. "John Claypool could be playing golf with O.J. next year if Taylor doesn't handle this extremely cautiously.''

Jane couldn't get to sleep.

She was about to drop off once when the smell of the dying embers of the fire took over her subconscious and she started half dreaming, half thinking about the huge wreck of a mansion burning down. Heart pounding, she got up and got a drink of water. Shelley mumbled in her sleep.

Jane went back to bed and minutes later was having another bad dream. She was walking in the woods around the camp, but everything had moved and changed. The Conference Center had turned into the Claypool mansion, with incongruous Spanish moss hanging from the trees in tatters. She tried to find the lodge. There were shuffling footsteps somewhere behind her. She'd be safe at the lodge, she thought. She could see lights in the distance and struggled through the underbrush, trying to get closer to them.

Somebody tapped her on the shoulder. She turned and found herself facing a huge falcon. Its eyes lit up like a Halloween pumpkin. She tried to turn and run, but her feet wouldn't move. The creature reached up with human hands and—horrors!—removed its own head and stuck it in her face.

Jane came suddenly awake, thrashing and trying to push the itchy, feathered monstrosity out of her face. Her watchband had caught in her hair and she pulled a chunk loose.

"Shelley!" she croaked. "Shelley, wake up!"

Shelley sat bolt upright, confused and disoriented. "What is it? What's wrong?"

"I know what the proof is!"

She leaped up and ran around Shelley's bed to turn on the bathroom light, instantly blinding both of them. "Call the lodge. Get Taylor back here."

"Are you really awake?" Shelley said, squinting. "Do you know what you're talking about?"

"Yes, I'm sure. It might be gone by now, but if it's not, we can hand the proof over to Taylor."

He arrived a few minutes later. Jane and Shelley

had flung on their clothes while they waited, and Jane had explained to Shelley what her dream had told her. Taylor looked rumpled and irritated, but cheered up considerably as Jane explained what she'd figured out. "I'll go roust Rycraft out of bed," he said.

"We're coming too," Jane declared.

They argued over it for a few minutes, but Jane and Shelley prevailed.

"And be sure you bring along the deputy with the monster flashlight," Shelley added.

The four of them—five, counting the flashlight—had to knock on Bob Rycraft's door for a few minutes. He finally opened it, blinking and confused. He wore only sweatpants and was scratching his stomach.

Before anyone else could speak, Jane said to the deputy, "Shine that monster on his stomach. Yes, it's a poison ivy rash, isn't it."

Everybody stared at Bob's washboard stomach. He kept blinking and trying to form a question, and they pushed into the cabin around him.

"Mr. Rycraft," Taylor said, "would you mind getting dressed and try to show us where you fell in the creek?"

"I—okay. I guess. Why?"

"Because we want to see if that costume mask is still there," Taylor explained.

Bob looked relieved. "Oh, that's all? No, it's not there. It's here. I thought my girls might have fun playing dress-up with it."

They followed him to the closet. "Don't touch it," Taylor said. He lifted it off the floor as if it were a

time bomb, walked gingerly to the middle of the
room, and delicately turned it over. The deputy
shined the monster flashlight into the inside of the
falcon hood. They all knelt and stared. The inside
was lined with a black felt material, and even without
a magnifying glass, they could see a few hairs stuck
to the felt. Several long, coppery ones that must have
belonged to the demonstrator from whom it was sto-
len, and a few short, straight, fair hairs.

"Yes!" Jane exclaimed. "And I'll bet that's why
John Claypool was scratching at his shin, too. He
and Bob ran into what's probably the only patch of
poison ivy on the campsite—John when he tried to
throw the mask and cloak in the creek, and Bob when
he fell in and found it."

"Don't anybody touch this," Taylor said, and to
the deputy added, "Call an ambulance. Tell them I
need a sterile sheet to wrap this in. It'll take weeks
for the DNA testing, but I think I've got enough now
to ask John Claypool some pretty pointed questions."

Twenty-three

❖ ❖ Sheriff Taylor and the deputy set out for John
  ❖   and Eileen Claypool's cabin. Bob stayed behind
to wait for the sterile sheet, and Jane and Shelley
followed the sheriff quietly and at a distance. If he
ordered them to stay away, they'd have to. If he
didn't notice them, it was a different matter.

Taylor went to the door and knocked. Jane and
Shelley lurked in the shrubbery at the end of the
short driveway of the cabin. There was one light on
inside, but no one came to the door. The van in the
driveway began slowly, silently rolling backwards.

"Sheriff!" Jane shouted, and she and Shelley
leaped out of the way of the vehicle.

Taylor whirled, spotted the van moving, and
leaped forward. "Hold it!"

Suddenly the engine started, the headlights went
on, and the van backed up into the road. Taylor ran
in front of it. With the headlights on, Jane could see
the top of the head of the driver.

Then the van shot forward, almost hitting Taylor,
who dived aside at the last second. The van skidded,

bumped into the sheriff's car, which was parked at the side of the road, and headed down the road toward the lodge.

Taylor leaped up from the mud and headed for his car. As the driver's door was stuck from the impact of the van, Shelley, Jane, and the deputy managed to get in first. The deputy, in the front passenger seat, leaned back and kicked the driver's door open. Taylor jumped in and gunned the engine. It took only seconds, but the van's taillights were well ahead of them.

"Where are they headed?" Jane asked as Taylor sped out.

He hadn't known they were in the car, and his head nearly swiveled off his neck. "Christ! What are you two doing back there?"

"I'm not sure," Jane said quite sincerely. She hadn't really thought it out, she'd just jumped in the car out of instinctive curiosity, not sensible reflection. "Where are we going?"

"Keep down," Taylor said. "I haven't got time to let you out. He's headed for the bridge. It's in place and I imagine he checked it out before trying to get away."

The road curved; the car slewed half sideways on some of the curves, but the van was moving even faster. Then, inexplicably, the sheriff let up on the gas pedal. Ahead of them and sharply to the right, Jane could see the bridge—a shiny new structure with floodlights at both ends, it was perfectly flat. As she stared at it, the van took the last curve, slid sickeningly, and kept on sliding sideways as it started across the temporary bridge. There was a shriek of

metal on metal as the back wheels dropped over the
sides of the overpass and the van's momentum kept
it moving. Sparks flew up from the raw meeting of
bridge and van undercarriage until the van stopped,
tottered like a seesaw for a moment, then gently,
gracefully, toppled backwards into the creek below.

By the time the sheriff got his vehicle stopped on
the brink of the creek, John Claypool had crawled
out and was in the water, clinging to the door of the
van and cursing horribly.

Shelley looked at Jane and said, in a dead calm
voice, "I don't *think* we want to ride back with him.
Let's walk."

She and Jane got out of the sheriff's car and
headed briskly back toward their cabin.

"Shelley," Jane said after they'd gone a little
ways, "I think this is about the only walk I've ever
actually enjoyed."

Those members of the committee who both sur-
vived the trip and remained at large attended a brief
meeting of the city council two weeks later. There
was no discussion and a quick, unanimous vote not
to contract with Benson Titus for a summer camp.
Liz was disappointed. She'd prepared a largish book-
let of her arguments against the proposal and hadn't
even mentioned murder, but nobody wanted or
needed to read it.

Marge, with a new hairstyle, and Eileen arrived
last and left first, and were polite but didn't seem the
least inclined to chat. Bob Rycraft brought two of
his little girls, and they headed for the ice cream
store within seconds of the vote. Al only popped his

head in the door for a moment, said, "I vote no," and disappeared.

Shelley and Jane were left with Liz.

"I took a casserole over to Marge," Liz said. "For the funeral. But I didn't know what to do about Eileen."

"She filed for divorce within hours of getting back home, you know," Shelley said.

"I saw that in the paper," Liz said. "Poor Eileen. Married to a murderer. Do you think she ever suspected?"

"Probably not until she came out of the shower and discovered he'd left her and was trying to run from the sheriff," Jane said. "She called me yesterday. Just to tell me she had no hard feelings about my role in the whole thing. Her son's come home, she says. Apparently he never got along with his father, which is why he chose to live so far away."

"And the senior Claypools? What's to become of them?" Liz asked.

"They had a nasty weekend, too, even before learning that one of their sons had killed the other," Jane said. "Eileen told me they managed to lock all the household help outside and decided since it was cold, it would be cheaper to warm up by burning some old furniture rather than turn on the furnace. Smoke was belching out some broken windows and the fire department had to break in. The experience must have pushed them both over the edge. Eileen's son, their only blood kin, has been appointed conservator. Popped them in a very nice nursing home and is trying to get the house in shape."

"Poor Eileen," Liz said. "And poor Marge. What-

ever will they do? I guess Marge will have to sell
the car dealership."

Jane said, "Don't be too sure of that. Eileen tells
me they're considering running it themselves.
They've signed up for some business management
and auto mechanics classes and are trying to find a
manager to run it while they get up to speed."

Liz narrowed her eyes. "Ah-hah! I heard Al on
the phone the other night, giving someone advice
about business managers. He wouldn't tell me who
he was talking to. I'll bet— Where is he, anyway?
Probably lost again."

"Liz," Jane said with a laugh, "there are only
about five rooms in this building! How could he
get lost?"

"I don't know. I've never understood it." She
picked up her stack of booklets and went in search
of him.

Shelley grinned. "I think getting lost is one of
Al's best skills. Are you free tomorrow?"

"Sure. What do you want to do?"

"I thought we might drive up and take a look at
the Claypool mansion. You never know—it might be
a great place for a summer camp."

Welcome to the World of
Jill Churchill

What could be more normal than a suburb just outside of Chicago? But the world of Jill Churchill is a world overrun by teenagers in suburban angst, mothers ruthlessly organizing car pools and committees, and next-door neighbors and best friends Jane Jeffry and Shelley Nowack, finders extraordinaire of fresh corpses.

Not that they're out looking for bodies, but murderous intent seems to run amok in their quirky community. And every time this duo stumbles on another deed, they can't help but sift through the gossip and scandal (much to the consternation of Jane's boyfriend, Detective VanDyne) over a good meal (nothing can dampen these ladies' appetites) and figure out who had motive enough to commit murder.

Award-winning, often funny, and always deadly, Jill Churchill's world is sure to keep you guessing.

Grime and Punishment

Jane and Shelley weren't always expert amateur crime solvers. When they discover their first body, Shelley's new cleaning lady, Shelley loses her legendary calm.

❖❖❖ In all the years they'd been friends, Jane had never known Shelley to lose her cool. But on the phone she'd been shrill, nearly hysterical. As Jane raced across the driveways and into the Nowacks' kitchen door, Shelley met her, wringing her hands and looking like death. Her face could have been painted white.

"I can't have heard you right," Jane panted.

"She's dead, Jane. It's horrible."

"Did you call the police and an ambulance?"

"Not yet. An ambulance won't help her."

"You don't know that, Shelley. It might be a heart attack or something. Maybe she just looks dead."

"Jane, believe me—" Shelley turned away and put her hand over her mouth, retching.

Jane ran up the stairs, skidding to a halt just inside the door to the guest room. She suddenly realized what Shelley meant. The cleaning lady was lying sprawled beside the bed, just inside the doorway.

Feet toward the door, face down, her head was turned sideways, and what Jane could see was sickening. The woman's skin was a mottled purple, her eyes bulged, and something fat and purplish and repulsive was sticking out of her mouth. It took Jane a few seconds to realize it was the woman's tongue.

The vacuum cleaner cord was twisted savagely around her bruised throat.

Jane's stomach heaved and she dashed for the bathroom. She clung to the sink, steeling herself. Then she rinsed her mouth, slapped some cold water on her face, and—carefully not looking toward the guest room—started downstairs. She had to lean on the banister for support. Her knees were shaking so badly she nearly tumbled forward twice.

Shelley was at the bottom of the stairs, and they fell into each other's arms. "Oh, my God, Shelley—" Jane whimpered. Shelley was crying. "We have to call the police. They'll take care of—of everything." She knew she was babbling, but she needed to say something.

"Oh, Jane . . ." Shelley moaned. "Take care of it? This is too awful. How could something so terrible happen?"

"That's for the police to figure out," Jane said. Since the normally bossy Shelley was on the verge of going to pieces, Jane felt the need to be confident. But her voice came out in a croaking manner that didn't sound like herself.

"Yes. Yes, you're right. I'll call," Shelley said, wiping her eyes on the sleeve of her elegant maroon suit. In other circumstances, Jane could have fainted from astonishment at seeing such a thing. Of course, in other circumstances, Shelley could never have done that.

"What shall I say?"

"I don't know," Jane said, following her back to the kitchen. They were moving along like children, clinging to each other as if afraid to let go.

Shelley picked up the phone, then put it back down. "I can't hear with that dishwasher going," she said. She looked down at the little light indicating the cycle. She went even whiter than before. "It's just on prewash . . ." she said tonelessly.

"So what? Just cancel the cycle— My God, Shelley!" Jane said, suddenly realizing the implications of this. "Did you start it before you found her?"

"No, she"—she gestured helplessly toward the stairs—"must have."

"Then that means she's only been dead a few minutes. Whoever did it might still be here."

They looked toward the family room, and suddenly the chairs and sofas became menacing—hiding places where murderers might be lurking. Jane grabbed Shelley's arm. "We'll call from my house."

"We shouldn't leave her. It doesn't seem decent."

"Decent! Nothing about this is decent, Shelley. Anyway, we can't do her any good now."

Holding hands like terrified schoolgirls, they ran across the adjoining drives and into Jane's kitchen.

A Farewell to Yarns

*Life is seldom as bucolic as it appears in this
scene, but between the number of heinous murders being perpetrated, Jane does manage to get
in some moments of normalcy (or at least as
normal as her life ever gets).*

December 10, 8:37 A.M.

❖ The Jeffry house in the suburbs of Chicago was
empty, but it was a hectic sort of emptiness. The
portable television in the kitchen was on the
"Today" show at top volume. Jane's ninth-grade
daughter, Katie, had turned it on in the desperate
hope of finding some tidbit of news with which to
complete her social studies assignment. Naturally,
she hadn't thought of turning it off before leaving
for school. Such things never occurred to Katie. From
upstairs, the sound of sixteen-year-old Mike's stereo
was blaring an extremely noisy Queen album. Mike
didn't set much store by turning things off, either.

The coffee maker was making a very peculiar burble because, in her haste to get her kids off to school,
Jane had slopped water on the heating element. The
furnace was going full blast, making the funny click-

ing sound Jane had been worrying about for a couple of days, and from the basement there was the sound of some lonely item of clothing with a metal button thrashing around in the dryer.

The kitchen phone was ringing insistently and was being ignored by the cat closest to it. He, a rotund gray tabby tom named Max, was standing in the sink fishing expertly in the garbage disposal for any little treasures that might not have been thoroughly disposed of. The faucet was dripping every few seconds on the back of his almost nonexistent neck, but it didn't seem to worry him. His counterpart, a sleek yellow item named Meow, was daintily cruising the breakfast room table for crumbs.

In the dining room a great shambling dog named Willard was barking his head off at the neighbor who walked the poodle by the house every morning. Willard had been soundly trounced once by the poodle and now spent a few refreshing moments every morning telling the interloper (from the safety of his own dining room) what would happen to him next time they met. Jane had to clean the low windows at least once a week because of his spitty morning barkfests.

Added to this at 8:38 was the rumble of Jane's car pulling into the driveway. "It's only a little hole in the muffler, Mom," Mike had assured her. Jane thought it sounded like the Concorde taking off every time she accelerated.

Jane Jeffry came in the outside kitchen door a moment later. Normally an attractive (though she didn't really think so) and well-groomed woman in her late thirties, this morning Jane was a wreck. Most of her blond hair was stuffed under a stocking cap that did more to emphasize than conceal its uncombed condition. She wore an antique and very tatty so-called mink she'd picked up at a garage sale several years earlier. Jane didn't really approve of wearing fur— her economics as well as ethics were offended by it—but this one looked like it came from an animal that *ought* to be extinct. The coat was a disgrace, and she knew it, but it was incredibly warm, just what she needed for driving winter morning car pools. With this unstylish garment, she wore jeans, a sweatshirt that said, "This is no ordinary housewife you're dealing with," and sheepskin slippers that she removed and shook the snow from into the sink— after hoisting Max out.

She leaned on the counter for a moment, looking around the kitchen with disgust. "This looks like white trash lives here, and it's your fault!" she told the cat. Then she bellowed at the dog, "Willard! I'll bring that poodle in here to beat you up if you don't stop barking this instant!"

There was a knock at the kitchen door, and Jane opened it to find her friend and next-door neighbor Shelley Nowack. A few snowflakes spangled Shelley's neat cap of dark hair and the velvet trim on her coat. In honor of the approaching holidays, she had a sequined Christmas tree brooch pinned to her lapel. Even in her distracted state, Jane noticed that Shelley's high-heeled boots were of exactly the same shade as her gloves and her purse. "How dare you look that good already."

"My God, Jane. What happened to you? You look like you've been savaged by a gang of bikers."

". . . which is roughly equivalent to being the mother of three kids. The electricity must have been out for an hour or so last night. We overslept. Why didn't you?"

"My alarm is battery powered. You should have one. Now I know what to get you for Christmas."

"I should have a lot of things. A housekeeper for starters. Then maybe an indulgent millionaire husband. Shelley, pour us some coffee, would you?"

A Quiche Before Dying

About the only good thing that comes out of the murders is the introduction of the hunky, younger Detective Mel VanDyne into Jane's life. Despite her interference in his investigations, Mel's finally asked Jane on a date, but, as can be expected, a dead person gets between them.

"Where are we off to?" Jane asked.

"I thought a Coke at McDonald's?"

"My kind of date," Jane said, then wondered if that had been the wrong thing to say. This wasn't exactly a date. It was more a casual pickup. She smiled at the thought of being picked up on the cusp of forty.

They got their drinks, then Mel drove to the mall, closed and deserted now, and stopped and turned off the car in the middle of the huge parking expanse. "Just thought I'd fill you in a bit," he said.

Jane very nearly said, "Gee, I hoped we were going to make out," but thought better of it for several reasons, the primary being that it was too close to the truth. The other thing that stopped her was the realization that they probably didn't call it that anymore, and he'd feel as if he were out with his mother. Instead, she asked, "Any more word on the poison?"

"Not yet," he said. "I guess once you get past the usual things to test for, you've got a lot of weird stuff to work through. But I did find out a few things I thought might interest you."

"Yes?"

"Ah . . . Jane, you do realize this is highly irregular, don't you?"

"What is? Sitting in a dark parking lot with a possible suspect? Taking an older woman out for a Coke?"

"Talking to you about this case. I hope you'll keep anything that I tell you in strict confidence."

Jane considered seriously. "Except for Shelley. She's my Watson. Or maybe I'm hers. I haven't figured that out yet."

He didn't answer for a long moment.

"You don't like Shelley, do you?" she asked.

"It's not that—"

"She's very blunt. She not only says what she thinks, lots of times she says what *I* think and didn't know," Jane said. "I know you feel we're being terribly callous about all this, and we probably are, but women *are* tough, Mel."

He turned and smiled at her, condescendingly, she thought.

Maybe it was because she was still smarting under Bob Neufield's earlier insult, maybe she'd reached some turning point in her life, but she suddenly threw caution to the winds.

"Look here, Detective VanDyne, I know you're a big, macho cop. You think you've seen the real nitty-gritty of life, and housewives are just dust-bunny-brains worrying about trivialities, but you've got it wrong. Any woman who's had to turn a baby upside

down and smack it nearly senseless to dislodge a
penny stuck in its throat knows as much of life and
death as you do—and in a much more personal way.
We learn a lot about life, because mothers live it
over again in each of their children. You've only
gone through teenage angst once. I've been though
it three times and still have one to go.''

She was on a roll and couldn't seem to stop. ''You
think cleaning and cooking and vacuuming are stupid, but they're important. They make a safe haven.
Those dumb, boring activities create a place where
kids know they're loved, and no matter how badly
life kicks them around, there's a place where somebody's doing her best to take care of them. You
wouldn't be the person you are if it weren't for a
caring mother. Men think they're so damned strong,
but for God's sake, haven't you ever stopped to think
who raised those strong men? Who taught them to
be what they are? Women, that's who! 'Ordinary'
women who clean up the cat shit and peel potatoes
and make damned Halloween costumes and still manage to do the most important job in the world—rais-
ing the next generation!''

Jane stopped raving, shocked at herself.

She cleared her throat, took a reckless swig of her
drink that nearly made her choke, and said, ''Sorry.
I must have suddenly been under the impression I
was running for office.''

Mel reached over, took the waxed cup from her
hand, and dropped it out on the pavement. Then he
put his hand on her cheek, leaned forward, and
kissed her.

The Class Menagerie

But as much affection as Jane might feel for Detective VanDyne, her first love will always be food. Here, Jane and Shelley try to figure out who is the practical joker at Shelley's high school reunion, and who is the murderer.

❖ "I'm starving. Have you got anything to eat here?" Shelley asked when Jane came back from yelling at the kids. "Preferably something salty and crunchy with the highest fat content possible?"

"Crackers and cheese?"

"Doesn't sound greasy enough, but it would do."

Shelley slumped on a kitchen chair while Jane got out snacks. "How about some hot chocolate, just to run the calorie count up?" Jane asked.

"Sounds wonderful."

While Jane worked, Shelley said, "I don't believe in cholesterol. I think within ten years they'll change their trendy little medical minds and say they were wrong all along and human beings really need as many saturated fats as they can knock back. They're already changing their minds about eggs."

"Interesting theory."

"Jane, consider this: human beings are carnivores.

The species developed in the jungle eating other creatures, finding eggs to steal, maybe eating the occasional plant, just for variety or out of desperation. I think red meat and eggs are the stuff of which humans are made.''

Jane set down a tray and two cups of steaming cocoa. She'd even put little marshmallows in the cups. "In that case, I'll be ready with my cabinets full of previously forbidden foods. Shelley, to get back to the subject at hand—this morning Mel was asking me about the practical jokes and he did something interesting that we ought to try.''

"What's that?''

"He made a list of the jokes and then went through it over and over, looking at them each time in a different way. Like, were they harmful? Who was the victim? Could they have a meaning? Did they require advance preparation?''

"Uh-huh. And did it lead him to any conclusion?''

"Not that I know of. Not then. But it's an interesting way of looking at things.''

"Okay . . . ?''

"So, let's do the same thing with the murder. We need to think about this in an organized, logical way.''

"All right. Where do we start?'' Shelley took an extremely unladylike bite of a cracker she'd slathered with a great deal of cheese.

"Well, how about this—if we agree that Lila was killed because she was blackmailing someone—''

"Do we know that?''

Jane thought for a minute. "No, actually we don't *know* it. It just seems extremely likely.''

"Likely isn't certain."

"No, but why else would somebody kill her?"

"Oh, any number of reasons, starting with the fact that she was an all-round obnoxious bitch."

"Yes, but there are a lot of those in the world, and most of them are still alive and kicking."

"Unfortunately," Shelley said with a grin.

"Okay, we can come back later to reexamine our basic premise. But for now, let's pretend that we *know* Lila was killed because she was blackmailing someone."

"Okay by me. Lead on, Sherlock." Shelley took a careful sip of her cocoa and closed her eyes appreciatively for a moment. "You have a great skill with premixed foodstuffs, Jane."

A Knife to Remember

Jane and Shelley are starstruck when a Hollywood movie starts filming in their backyards. But their rose-tinted glasses are mostly transparent as they view this particularly distasteful prelude to murder.

❖❖❖ Their conversation was cut short by the entrance of the director into the craft service area—and "entrance" it was. Roberto Cavagnari was a stocky little tractor of a man with dark, flashing eyes, designer jeans, and a flamboyant green velvet poncho that would have looked effeminate on anybody less aggressively male. He didn't walk; he strutted. He didn't speak; he proclaimed. Underlings schooled around him like minnows around a handsome, glittering trout.

"Call the weatherman," he ordered in what sounded to Jane suspiciously like a fake Italian accent. "I won't have overcast sky today." Jane wondered if he really supposed that weathermen ordered the weather rather than merely reporting it. A toady ran to do his bidding.

"Mister Cavagnari, if I could just have a word wi—" somebody said.

But the underling's request was lost in the next declaration. "I will have coffee. Mocha. Extra sugar," Cavagnari announced. Another assistant rushed to do the maestro's bidding, but he stopped her with an authoritative snap of his stubby, beringed fingers. "No, I will prepare it myself so it's done correctly," he said in the tones an empress might have used to say she'd do her own mending. Underlings fell back, nearly bowing, as he approached the snack table.

"*Ja, mein herr,*" Shelley said under her breath.

"I think you've got the wrong country," Jane whispered. "I think we're supposed to be chanting, '*Duce! Duce!*'"

Shelley laughed and Cavagnari whirled and glared at them for a moment before turning back to the preparation of his mocha coffee.

A second later he bellowed, "Jake! Jake! Here she is, my watch! I told you to look here."

Jake materialized at his side. "I did look for it here. Not half an hour ago."

"You did not use your eyes, Jake. It was here, beneath a chip wrapper."

"I am very good at seeing objects! I searched thoroughly," Jake said firmly. "It was *not* here."

"But you see? Here . . . just here before my eyes." He slipped the watch on.

"I tell you it was not—"

"Enough, Jake! I have spoken. It is done."

Jake subsided, obviously furious at having both his judgment and his eye for details questioned, but apparently unwilling to anger Cavagnari further. His eyes narrowed and he looked around the group as if daring anyone else to criticize him. Then his expression turned deeply thoughtful.

Cavagnari discoursed briefly on the proper way to prepare his coffee, most of his audience pretending rapt attention. Then, when it was done to his satisfaction, he sipped and said, kissing his fingertips and offering them to heaven, "Perfect! Now, we will do the close-ups of scene fourteen, then luncheon."

He swept away, underlings trailing like the train of a coronation gown.

"Wow!" Shelley breathed. "That's an extraordinary display of ego run amok."

From Here to Paternity

Jane and Shelley aren't exactly workout addicts. So when they go on a vacation where strenuous physical exercise is required, it takes them a while to "warm up" to it. In this scene our duo is set to ski—for the first time. But luckily the Colorado mountains also offer great après ski meals.

❖❖ "Okay, here's the deal," Shelley pronounced.
"We're going clear to the top of the hill. Then we're coming back down by whatever method works out best and no matter how many times we fall along the way. Then we're retiring. Just think, for the rest of our lives we can say We Have Skied. And nobody will ever be able to say, 'But you must try it once.' So we'll never have to do it again."

"Sounds like a good plan to me. Is there food at the end of this scenario? You didn't mention food."

"There's a huge lunch, Jane."

"Okay."

They started laboriously stairstepping their way up the hill. After about ten minutes, during which she had to look at her feet to make sure they were doing the right thing, Jane stopped. "Jeez! We should be clear to the top by now. And we're still at the bottom.''

"Keep going, Jane," Shelley said. "Think about lunch.''

"There's that person again," Jane said, shading her eyes and looking up at the top of the hill.

"Which person?"

"I don't know. Just a person I keep seeing. He has cameras and binoculars. A nature nut, I imagine.''

"Jane, stop talking.''

They stairstepped some more, and it was Shelley this time who wanted to stop. "Look at that! We're nearly halfway up the hill.''

"We could just go from here.''

"No, we're going to the top. Once. Look at the cute snowman.''

"Hadn't you noticed him before? He appeared overnight.''

"What's he got on his head?''

"I think it's supposed to be a crown.''

"I know, but what is it really?''

"I dunno. Maybe one of those sort of fluted fruit bowls? Remember the gold plastic ones we used for that PTA fund-raising party with a Tropical Holiday theme? To quote a friend of mine, stop talking!''

After two more rest stops, they reached the top of the hill and sat down to get their breath. "Wow! This is neat up here," Jane gasped. "Look, the whole resort's laid out like a map. You should have brought a camera along. You could have taken a picture for Paul so when he gets home and wonders just where the various buildings and wings are, you'd have it. Are you ready to go?''

"Not yet. I'm never coming here again for the rest of my life, so I want to appreciate it for a few minutes. The snowman looks weird from the back. Just the cape and crown showing."

Jane was gazing around behind them. "The Indians who were demonstrating said there was a graveyard up here. It doesn't look like that to me."

"Jane, it's covered with snow. How would you know? You expect to see a mausoleum or a totem pole or something sticking up?"

"Hmmm. You have a point. It's certainly flat enough to make a good cemetery. Looks like somebody took a gigantic knife to it and sliced the top off. You could land a 747 along here."

Shelley was hoisting herself to her feet. "Speaking of landing, are we ready to take off?"

"I guess so. It sure looks a lot steeper from the top."

"How are we going to do this? One at a time all the way down?"

"Okay. Who goes first?"

"I do. I want to get this over with."

Shelley took a deep breath, turned her skis forward, and started gently drifting away. She picked up speed gradually until, apparently feeling it was too much of a good thing, she sat down suddenly, plowing a bit of a trench before she came to a complete stop. She yelled up to Jane, "Come this far and we'll go the rest of the way together."

Jane set out, cleverly charting a course a little farther left than Shelley had gone so that she wouldn't run over her. The first few minutes were okay. She started going a little faster, discovered that she could actually breathe at the same time she skied. And a little faster yet. She tried toeing-in to slow herself, but that just made her veer more to the left. Maybe, she thought frantically, it was toe-out. She glanced down at her feet, which was how she made her fatal mistake. When she looked back up a second later, she realized she was headed toward the woods. Specifically, straight for the snowman just on the edge of the woods.

She tried to sit down, but was leaning too far forward. *Crouch!* she told herself frantically, but she was so tense that her knees just wouldn't get the message.

With a terrific mental effort, she made her legs go limp and sat down. By that time she was moving so fast that she kept going for another five feet, sending up a spray of snow. The thing that finally stopped her was the snowman. She didn't so much crash into it, for her speed had diminished considerably, as bump into it firmly. Very firmly.

The snowman's head rolled off, sending the crown/bowl spinning across the snow.

"Jane! Are you all right?" Shelley yelled from someplace off to her right.

"I'm okay," Jane said, trying to stand up. Where had her skis gone? she was wondering. If they'd buried themselves in the snow, how would she ever find them? Still shaky from her adventure, she leaned on the snowman, placing her gloved hand where its head had been. But as she did so, the whole front section of the snow crumbled away in a slab.

And there, inside the snowman where there should have been nothing but more snow, was the body of Bill Smith.

Silence of the Hams

*By the time their seventh murder mystery rolls
around, Jane and Shelley have become so good
at theorizing, they've got it down to a precise
mathematical formula that makes perfect sense
to them.*

❖ "Okay," Shelley said in her organizational
voice. "Here's the situation: X finds Y dead on
the floor—"

"Apparently dead," Jane interrupted.

"Good. Yes, that might make all the difference.
X finds Y sprawled on the floor. Maybe dead. Maybe
unconscious. Pushes a heavy thing over on him, making it look like Y was murdered. So, what could the
reasons be?"

"Sheer frustration," Jane said. "X hated Y,
planned to kill him, and is furious to think somebody
else got to it first and lashes out in a fit of pique."

"Okay, that's one," Shelley said. "Sheer hatred.
X hated Y, but couldn't take any action against him,
so when he sees him helpless for once, he's over-
come by the impulse to dish out vengeance. And
even if he knew for sure that Y was already dead,

that hatred might just need the outlet of pretending to kill him."

"A bit more baroque," Jane said as if evaluating a painting. "How's this: X finds Y lying dead on the floor—doesn't necessarily even know or care who it is, but has a rabid hatred for Z—"

"Z?" Shelley asked indignantly.

"Let me finish. X hates Z and thinks by pushing the rack over on Y, he can blame it on Z."

"Who could Z be?" Shelley asked, still apparently resentful of the introduction of this new character.

"The first person who comes to mind is Conrad, just because it's his deli. Or maybe X planned to claim later that he'd seen Z leave the room just before the crash."

"If that were the case, why didn't X ever make such an accusation?" Shelley asked.

As serious as the subject really was, Jane felt a sense of ghoulish amusement take over. "Try this one then: X knows Y is having an affair with Z and was once married to Q, who is trying to haul him into court to testify in a drug-running case against P—"

"—and S knew all about it and was threatening to tell M, who feared that K would hear about it and All Would Be Revealed!" Shelley finished. "I like it, Jane. Mel, we've solved it. You can probably still make your arrest this evening if you hurry."

Mel stared at them and then spoke very slowly and deliberately. "I thank all that is holy that you two didn't go into law enforcement."

Murder Is on the Menu
at the Hillside Manor Inn
Bed-and-Breakfast Mysteries by
MARY DAHEIM
featuring Judith McMonigle Flynn